Sugar Walls

Sugar Walls

A novel by
BRITTANI WILLIAMS

Q-Boro Books
WWW.QBOROBOOKS.COM

An Urban Entertainment Company

Published by Q-Boro Books
Copyright © 2007 by Brittani Williams

ISBN-13: 978-1-933967-26-4
ISBN-10: 1-933967-26-9
LCCN: 2006937336

First Printing December 2007
Printed in the United States of America

10 9 8 7 6 5 4 3 2

Cover Copyright © 2006 by Q-BORO BOOKS, all rights reserved.
Cover layout/design by Candace K. Cottrell
Cover photo by Jose Guerra; models Shauna Faith, Jay Reed, and
Tiffany Harris
Editors: Andrea Blackstone, Candace K. Cottrell, Latoya Smith

Q-BORO BOOKS
Jamaica, Queens NY 11434
WWW.QBOROBOOKS.COM

A few seconds of pleasure can lead to a lifetime of pain . . .

Sugar Walls

Prologue

"I'm sorry, Mommy! I'll make sure she stays out of trouble. I promise," I cried.

"I know you will, and I want you to remember this so there won't be any more mistakes!" my mother yelled before shoving me into the tub full of hot water.

"Please don't, Mommy," I pleaded. I just wanted to go to bed and forget all about today.

"It's too late for that!" She pulled her long, black, leather belt through each loop of her denim jeans in seconds.

I blacked out once she began to hit me across my back and behind with the belt. I couldn't cry because I was in so much pain. I held it in, which only fueled her fire and caused me to receive more hits across the back. After my father came home and heard me in the bathroom screaming and begging her to stop, he entered the bathroom and grabbed her by the arm.

"That's enough!" he yelled.

"I don't think she gets the point. She hasn't even shed a tear!" she yelled.

"Look, I said that's enough. Get her out of that tub and let her go to bed; she has school tomorrow," he instructed.

"Come on! Go take your behind to bed, and you better remember what I said too," she yelled, before pushing me out of the bathroom.

I ran out of the bathroom and into the bedroom where my sister was lying down pretending to be sleep. I put on my nightgown after drying of and after crawling under the sheets I began to cry hoping that I wasn't loud enough to be heard by my mother.

"Are you OK?" my sister whispered across the room.

"What do you think? No, I'm not OK!"

"Well, why are you mad at me?" she asked.

"Because it's all your fault that she beat me. If you would have stayed by my side when we walked from school, this would have never happened. She told me to keep an eye on you and even after I told you that, you wandered off."

"Well, I'm sorry. I won't ever do it again! OK?"

"I hope not," I said, turning over and closing my eyes. I said a silent prayer and thanked God for my father walking in at the right time. That was the first time that I had even been beaten so badly, and I hoped that it would be the last. I begged my sister to stay out of trouble because I would take the blame for it. Sisters are supposed to stick together, and if knowing her actions would cause me harm wasn't enough to keep her straight, then I didn't know what else would.

I drifted off to sleep within minutes, and in the morning my mother acted as if last night never happened. I couldn't pretend because my back and behind were still stinging from the lashes on them. It was hard for me to even sit down and eat my cereal that morning. I was ten and even though I was more advanced than any ten year old in my school, I couldn't understand why a mother would hurt their child the way that she had hurt me.

I believed that my father was my savior, but that would be the last time that he intervened when I was being abused. The hits never stopped, and each time he would turn his head and ignore it. I would never forget that and I would never forgive him for it either.

Chapter 1

Sugar's the Name

It was cold, dark, snowing, and lonely as I lay tied up with no idea where I was. I could feel each of my limbs freezing one by one. I could barely even speak, let alone scream for help. No one could help me; no one even knew where I was except the bastard that put me here. I could hear random noises in the background—police sirens, horns beeping, music playing—but all of those sounds were distant and too far away for my weakened voice to be heard. There was a blanket over my entire body, and I didn't have enough energy to sit up and see where I was.

The way that I had mapped out my life, I never thought that it would land me there. I had a plan A, B, and C, none of which included being beaten, tied up, and left for dead in the snow. That cold, dark night led me to reflect back to how I got there and how it all began. It also made me wonder if I could have done anything to prevent it or done anything different to make my life turn out the way that I had originally planned.

I thought back, and I should have known I was cursed from the beginning with a name like Sugar Alise Clark. I always wondered how I got a name like Sugar, and the only explanation was that I reminded her of the drugs she called Sugar. Did that mean I ruined her life? Did that mean I was that bad that I could be compared to a drug? I was born to an alcoholic, drug-addicted mother and a deadbeat, drunk-ass father. I'm surprised DHS even allowed them to bring me home from the hospital! It's amazing how the things that you think a child should be taken away for are totally opposite of the things that they are really taken away for.

My mother Elaine was once a beautiful woman, far tucked under the tired appearance that she carried now. Pictures of her were the only proof of her past beauty, because the way that she looked now was the only way that I had ever seen her.

Elaine was born and raised in Brooklyn, New York, but she moved to Philadelphia after graduating high school to attend Temple University. Her college life was short-lived when she dropped out after only two semesters. She decided that college was too hard and took too much energy to end up making less that someone with no college education. She opted to stay in Philadelphia after meeting my father Ron at an off-campus party. They hit it off quickly, but their relationship was anything but perfect. I never knew what she saw in him or even what he saw in her for that matter. They were total opposites, but they also say that opposites attract. They argued constantly, and there were numerous occasions when the police had to be called out to the apartment when their auguring escalated to blows.

Ron worked at any place he could make a quick dollar. He never had a real job, just handyman work and other things of that sort. He would cut grass in the spring and summer, rake leaves in the fall, and shovel snow in the winter—your neighborhood hustle man.

How my mom fell in love with him I'll never know, but I do know that he was a big factor in her downfall. Soon after moving in with him, they began drinking heavily and snorting cocaine on a regular basis. Neither of them could keep a steady job, so we basically lived in poverty. My mother collected welfare from the government but never really used it to support us, she mainly used it to support he drug habits. She would sell the food stamps to buy drugs. Our parents were barely able to feed us because their drug habits were more important to them than feeding us. I was always ashamed of my mother and father, and there were many times that I wished that I had never even been born. No child should ever feel that way, but unfortunately I did.

I was their first born, with my sister Mya to follow. Mya and I were best friends growing up, close as two sisters could be. It wasn't until I realized that she didn't feel the same way I felt about her that our close friendship faded away.

I wasn't fast like most young girls growing up; I didn't loose my virginity until I was eighteen. I was never the girl that stood out; the guys in school never paid me any attention. Mya, on the other hand, received so much attention that she didn't know how to handle it. At the young age of fifteen, Mya had her first child. Marlo was one of the unlucky men that my sister slept with— unlucky meaning the fool that got her pregnant. See, Mya had a reputation far from a good one. She was branded the "neighborhood booty" because most dudes in the hood could get some from her anytime they wanted. Especially if the money was right.

Marlo was different. He was from South Philly, so he

had never had the opportunity to sit in on any conversations where Mya's sexual favors were the topic. She met Marlo after leaving WOW skating rink on a Saturday night. Marlo noticed Mya and a group of females including me waiting on the R bus to get back home. Marlo drove up in a brand new Mazda Millennia, black with extra dark tint in all of the windows.

Mya stood about 5'5 at the time, and she wore her hair short and spiked. She lined her lips perfectly with brown lip liner and applied her cherry lip-gloss, making her lips shine. Her body was one like Halle Berry; even at the age of fourteen she mirrored that of an adult woman. Dancing in her short denim mini, there was no way that Marlo could resist.

He pulled into the gas station behind the bus stop where we were standing and beeped his horn before rolling down his window. Not calling anyone directly, Mya quickly switched over to the car, automatically assuming that he was beeping the horn for her.

"What's up, sexy? What's a fine-ass girl like you doing waiting at the bus stop? If that nigga you were fucking was a real man, he'd be picking you up, or better yet, he'd buy you a car so you wouldn't have to wait on nobody's damn bus!"

"Well, I don't have a man, so that's why I'm out here," she said in a sexy tone.

"All of that can change if you want it to."

"Oh, really!"

"Really, if you fuck with a real man and stop playing with these kids!"

"Well, I'm down for whatever! I need a real man in my life," she said, bending over further into the car so that her entire ass was nearly hanging out of the short skirt she was wearing.

"Let me give you a ride so we can talk more. I'll tell you all about what I can do for you on the way."

"Cool, let me go tell my girls I'm leaving with you."

"All right, don't have me waiting too long!"

"I promise I won't," she said before walking back to where we were standing.

Angry, I spoke, "What the hell is wrong with you, Mya? You don't even know him!"

"I will know him by the end of the night," she laughed.

"You are so dumb, Mya! Do you even know his name? And how are you going to leave me to go home by myself. It's 10:00 at night."

"You'll be all right. I haven't had sex in a while and I need a hook-up! Sorry, I'll see you tonight. Cover for me with Mom."

"As if she'll notice you are not there anyway. She'll be too busy getting high. And then be pissed at me tomorrow," I yelled before she turned to walk away.

"Well then it's settled, I'll see you later. I promise I won't stay out all night so she won't even notice that I didn't come in," she said before running off.

"Mya!" I yelled.

Mya entered the car without even turning around to acknowledge me. I was pissed; this wasn't the first time that she left me hanging like that and at that moment I felt that it wouldn't be the last time either. That night, I made it home safely though I ran fast from the bus stop, afraid that I would be attacked. Entering our small, roach infested two-bedroom apartment I found my mother asleep on the living floor. There was a glass pipe or a glass "dick" as they call it less than two feet away from her. I went into my bedroom as I usually did, put on my headphones, and drifted off to sleep. I learned after many sleepless nights to wear the headphones to block out the drunken arguments between my mother and father, or the loud-ass sexual episodes they would have after getting high. I listened to my music to block out the realities of my world. The music made it easier for me to sleep at night.

Mya never came home that night, and as usual I was the one who received the punishment. Being slapped, waking me out of my sleep was something I was used to. Since I was older, and I was responsible. My mother made sure I knew if Mya messed up, I would be punished for it.

"Mom, what are you hitting me for?" I yelled, shocked by the blow to my stomach.

"Where the fuck is Mya? She didn't come home last night. How many times do I have to tell you to make sure she brings her ass home!" she yelled.

"Mom, I tried, but she didn't listen." I cried.

"You didn't try hard enough. Next time you are really going to make sure that she comes home or I'm going to fuck you up for not doing what you were told!" she yelled, pointing her index finger in my face.

"Why do I get in trouble for her?" I asked, petrified.

"Don't question me, I pay the bills in this muthafucker, and until you get your own, don't ask me shit! I make the rules. Don't you ever forget that!" she yelled, leaving the bedroom and slamming the door.

I sat there and cried as I usually did. Mya was never punished for anything, only me and I was the stand-up student, how ironic is that? I came home every night; Mya maybe came home once or twice a week. Therefore I was punished five or six days a week. I was slapped, punched, kicked, and spit on for things that I didn't even do. The abuse had only gotten worse the older we both got. Since Mya thought that she was more of an adult each year and could get away with anything, it caused more abuse to me.

That afternoon Mya strolled in after twelve when she

knew my mother would be out buying her drug and liquor supply for the night. I was in my room studying.

"Hey, did Mom notice that I was gone?"

"Of course she did. I thought you weren't going to stay out all night. You know she came in here hitting me this morning. Mya, why do you always do that when you know what she's going to do to me?"

"Sorry, Sugar, but I was having so much fun with Marlo and I didn't want to leave," she spoke, before kicking off her shoes.

"Marlo! So that's his name? Did you have sex with him?" I asked angrily.

"Of course I did. I needed some sexual healing!" she said, laughing.

"I don't think it's funny, Mya!" I yelled.

"Well, I do! I enjoyed myself. And quit yelling before Mom hears you"

"Whatever," I said before tuning her out.

I learned early on that Mya didn't care about anyone but Mya. Too bad for me that I cared about her. The following day I went to school as usual and to my part-time job at Bloomingdale's afterwards. I loved my job; it was the only time I was ever able to be around designer clothing. I even tried different outfits on some days just to pretend that I was actually going to buy them.

I dealt with the rude customers, and it didn't bother me half as bad as the treatment that I received at home. I was constantly looked down on for working in a department store, but I didn't care because I was working to save money for my college education.

I caught the bus to work and greeted everyone as I clocked in. I felt like today was going to be a long day. I normally worked in the children's department, but I was placed in the women's shoe department due to a call-out.

This day was the day that would eventually change my life, and though I didn't find out until weeks later I should have predicted it. I was summoned by a customer for help, and I instantly noticed her beauty. This woman stood about 5'9, perfect shape and flawless face. Her make-up was perfect as if it had been professionally applied. I tried not to stare, but I was mesmerized. I jumped at the chance to meet her even if only to get the shoes that she wanted from the stock room.

"Hi, how can I help you?" I asked nervously.

"Can I see these in a size 7?" She passed me three pairs of Marc Jacobs pumps.

"Sure, I'll be right back!" I said, smiling before going in the back to search for the shoes. I rushed because I didn't want her to get impatient. Once I was back on to the sales floor she was sitting down, waiting for me to return.

"OK, I've found all three. Just let me know if you need anything else."

"Would you mind giving me your opinion?"

"No. Not at all," I said anxiously.

She tried on each pair and I told her how good each pair looked on her feet. I wasn't gay by far, but to be honest, she was the prettiest woman I had ever seen. She thanked me and ended up purchasing all three pairs of shoes, totaling $1,195.

"Thanks a lot! What's your name?" she asked.

"Sugar!"

"Is that you real name?"

"Yeah."

"Did you ever think about modeling or anything? You have a really pretty face."

"Not at all! No one has ever told me I was pretty," I said, shocked by the comment. My mother told me that I was her ugliest child and that no man would ever look my way.

Her predictions had been accurate thus far, because this mystery customer was the first person to ever speak those words to me.

"Well, here's my card. Call me and maybe I can hook you up with a job, then you can afford to buy the same stuff that you sell!" She smiled.

"OK, thank you Ms . . ."

"Dyna, the name's Dyna. I'll look forward to hearing from you." She smiled and reached out to shake my hand and give me her business card.

"OK," I said, putting the business card into my back pants pocket.

I continued work, still in pain from the blow I received from my mother the day before. I caught the bus home and dreaded going in, afraid of what would be waiting on me when I got there. I never knew what to expect going home. Mya went to a different school than I did, so I was never sure if she went to school or not. Every night when I would come home from work I was afraid that I would be beaten if Mya had missed school that day. I entered the apartment and found Mya and my father sitting on the sofa watching the television.

"Hey, baby! How was work?" my father asked.

"Fine," I said blandly before walking into my bedroom.

My father, unlike my mother, never abused me. Though he smoked the same amount of crack that my mother did, his attitude was totally different. I loved my father, but was always afraid to show it because of my mother's jealous actions. If he showed us any attention when she was around, we were sure to be punished for it later. Mya was always closer to my father than I was. I guess that she wasn't as afraid of my mother as I was, because her beatings were never as brutal as mine. I entered my room and followed my daily routine of homework and then shortly after fell to sleep.

I went to school the following day as usual. I went to all of my classes and sat and ate lunch alone waiting for Marissa to arrive. I didn't have many friends—truthfully I only had one true friend and that was Marissa. Marissa was normal, nothing really striking about her appearance. She was raised by her mother who worked as a maid most of her life. The money that her mother made was never really enough to supply Marissa and her siblings with good clothing. They were forced to wear clothes from random thrift shops and hand-me-downs. I met her in fifth grade, and we had been best friends ever since. There were many times that we were in fights because people constantly picked on both of us. Me, I wasn't wearing thrift shop clothing, but I wasn't pretty and I was overweight. Plus the fact that I always had a bruised face or busted lip from my mother didn't help. Marissa was pretty, but she didn't stand out because of her attire, and she was ridiculed constantly because of it. We would both fight for each other, and never thought twice about doing anything different. I sat at the table for a few minutes before she decided to show up at lunch.

"What's up, what took you so long?" I asked.

"I had to finish up my test, sorry! No one messed with you did they?"

"No, I'm fine. You know I got in trouble this weekend for Mya again."

"You know, if I was you I would beat her up every time I got in trouble for her. That's crazy that she doesn't even care."

"Mya only cares about herself. Maybe if I didn't care about her it wouldn't bother me as much."

"Well you need to be more like her, stop caring!"

"It's easy to say that, but she is my little sister."

"I know, but it's a shame. Well, you'll be graduating soon and you can go to college and be rid of all of their crazy asses!" she said, laughing.

The next three months flew by. My mother and father didn't even attend my graduation, but I didn't care. I was proud of myself if no one else was. After graduating and returning home to the apartment, my mother said that she forgot all about it. I knew that was a lie and I also knew that my father didn't come because my mother wouldn't allow him to. I began working full-time during the weeks after school was over. My daily routine was soon without any incident until Mya decided to get pregnant. I came home from work to our small two-bedroom apartment and found my mother sitting on the sofa. I figured my father was probably out hustling up some more drug money. I sat my bag down and was instantly approached by my mother.

"Did you know that your sister was pregnant?" she yelled.

"What?"

"You heard me, your little ho-ass sister got herself pregnant. Where the hell were you? Too busy worrying about yourself to do what I told you to do."

"Mom, I am working to go to college."

"Fuck that! You ain't ever going to be shit anyway, so you are wasting your time. I told you to be responsible for your sister, very simple and you couldn't do that. How the fuck do you think that you will finish college?" She began laughing.

"I will finish, and I don't find anything funny. Mya is old enough to be responsible for herself."

She smacked me making me fall to the floor. "Who the fuck are you talking to?" she yelled.

I got up off the floor angry. I could no longer hold back all of the built up anger that I carried all of those years that I had been abused. I could no longer be subjected to her abuse for things that I didn't do. I stood there rubbing my swollen lip as she yelled more obscenities in my face. I balled up my fist, and after two many "bitches" that she called me, I began punching her repeatedly. She fell to the floor with me on top of her, and I continued beating her until I was exhausted. Her emaciated frame was nothing compared to mine. I jumped up, grabbed my bag, and ran out of the apartment crying. I was hurt because it had been going on too long. I had enough at that point and I didn't care what happened to my mother after that. I wanted her out of my life.

I took a little money out of my bank account and stayed at a hotel that night. The hotel was nothing spectacular, but it was much more than the apartment that I had shared with my family. I took a long hot bath, and I quickly fell to sleep on the queen-sized bed that was much more comfortable than the twin size mattress on the floor that was my bed before. That was the first night that I didn't have to wear my headphones to block out the noise around me. That was my first peaceful sleep, and I had waited long enough to have it.

Chapter 2

Good for the Gander . . .

I woke up the next morning and calculated my funds. I figured out that with the amount of money that I had saved all that I could spare was about three more days of stay at the hotel. I looked through my purse counting every nickel, dime and penny to add that to my total spending amount. While searching through my purse, I came across the business card that I had got from Dyna at Bloomingdale's. The card read, DYMES EXOTIC ESCORT SERVICES. I had never read the card after she had given it to me, so the nature of her business shocked me.

I knew that the escort business was nothing but a fancy name for prostitution. I now knew how she could afford the nice things that she had. I decided to give her a call, hoping that maybe she could help me out. Dialing the number I was nervous, it rang twice before someone answered.

"Dymes. How can I help you?" the woman spoke

"Hi, is Dyna available?" I asked nervously.

"May I ask who's calling and what's the nature of this call?"

"My name is Sugar. She gave me her business card months ago and told me to give her a call."

"OK, please hold."

After a beep and a few rings, "Hello!"

"Hi, this is Sugar. Is this Dyna?"

"Hi Sugar, I'm surprised to hear from you. I gave you that card so long ago."

"So you remember me? I just found your card today in my purse."

"How could I forget a name like Sugar?" she giggled before speaking again. "Well, do you want to come down and talk? I know things must not be shaping up for you if you are calling me."

"Yeah, I can come down. I'm off work today, so what time is good?"

"As soon as you can get here is fine with me."

"OK."

She gave me the directions to her business before hanging up. Though I was a little nervous about the meeting because I wasn't sure what to expect, I was very anxious to find out. I quickly got dressed and caught three buses and walked five blocks to reach the Dymes headquarters. It was a small building located in Center City. The building had a storefront with the name DYMES CLOTHING on the banner. I entered the clothing store and asked the sales woman where I could find Dyna. After making a phone call, she directed me to a door at the back of the store that lead to stairs. I walked up the steps and knocked on the door. I was greeted by Dyna, dressed from head to toe in designer clothing. I dreamed of the day I would be able to don the type of clothing she wore, but the small amount of money I was paid at Bloomingdale's would never be enough to afford them.

"Hey, girl. I was just talking about you. Come in. Sugar, this is Meeka. Meeka, meet Sugar."

"Hello!" I said, giving a slow wave.

"What's up?" Meeka said, giving me an evil grin.

I wasn't sure what that look was about, but I really wasn't concerned with it at the time.

"Would you excuse us, Meeka? I'll finish up with you when I'm done."

"Cool!" Meeka said before leaving the room.

"Have a seat," Dyna instructed. "So, how old are you Sugar?"

"I'm eighteen."

"So, what made you call me?"

"I had a big fight with my mom and I left home. I decided to leave for good to work on myself."

As I sat there recounting the story, I held back my tears. I hated the fact that my family was so dysfunctional, and it was embarrassing telling someone that I didn't even know. At the time I felt like I didn't have anyone else to talk to, and I hoped she would somehow be able to help me.

"Well, I can help you, but I don't know what kind of help you are willing to receive."

"I need a place to stay. I'm staying at a hotel now. I need clothes, shoes, I don't have anything."

"Well, I can help you with that. It's nothing, but what will you do for me in return?" she responded, while giving a slight grin.

"I'm a virgin, so I definitely can't be an escort," I quickly admitted before she got the wrong idea. I needed help, but if that was the only way that I could get it, I surely wasn't interested.

Laughing, "I didn't expect that. I could put you on my promotion team. You can go around passing out business cards and flyers, so some of the top neighborhood hustlers can be targeted. I have a range of clients, and I mostly get my high-end clients online, but the hustlers never go online. Shit, some of them don't even own computers. My business front is the clothing store and adult entertainment. The online thing has been working so far, but I need more men to know about the services."

"That's all? I can do that. That's not a problem at all."

"OK, well here's my American Express card. I'll have one of the girls drive you to the mall and you can buy what you need."

"Are you serious?" I was shocked because I couldn't believe that she had given me a job so quickly, let alone giving me her credit card to spend money freely.

"Of course. I believe in you. You might make me a lot of money one day. I'm also going to let you stay at my crib too, but we'll talk about that later."

I wasn't sure what she meant by that, but I was so wrapped up in my excitement that I ignored her comment. "Well how much am I supposed to spend?"

"Two or three G's. Whatever, it's cool. I'll get Nina to drive you," she said before calling Nina, the woman who greeted me in the clothing store downstairs.

I thanked Dyna in advance for all of her help. Nina waited for me and showed me to her car. I was still in disbelief. I couldn't really wrap my mind around the fact that someone was actually being nice to me and that they actually cared. Growing up with a family where you never really mattered, coming into this was definitely a treat. Once in the car, Nina began a conversation with me.

"So, where did you meet Dyna?"

"While I was at work, at Bloomingdale's. How about you?"

"She's my cousin."

"Do you work as an escort?"

"No, I work in the store and do runs for her. She pays me good money for it though."

"That's cool."

"So, how old are you? Because you look like a baby."

"I'm eighteen. I just graduated from high school. I'm planning on going to college."

She began laughing, "That's a good dream!"

"What's so funny about that?"

"Nothing, except the fact that every girl that works for Dyna including Dyna had the same dream. Look where they are now!"

Ignoring that comment, I asked, "Meeka, who is she to Dyna?"

"That's her girlfriend!"

"Her girlfriend? Dyna's gay?"

"She's bisexual, like most of the girls here."

"Wow, that's crazy." I would have never suspected a woman as beautiful as Dyna would be sexing another woman.

"Get used to it, baby girl. It's a lot more to come!"

I wondered what Nina meant by the comments that she made. I knew for a fact that I was going to finish school. I felt like this experience was just a stepping-stone, helping me to save the money that I needed for my education. Nina and I drove to the King of Prussia Mall to begin my shopping spree. Nina and I talked the entire time that we shopped. The experience was weird because I had never been out shopping with a friend before. Though I had just met Nina, I felt that eventually her and me would be really close.

The shopping outing lasted about three hours and I spent about $2,500. I bought every designer thing that I had dreamed of. I did most of my shopping in Bloomingdale's courtesy of my employee discount.

After leaving the mall, we returned to the store, and Dyna and I left to go to her house. It was a beautiful five-bedroom house in Delaware County. Every room was filled with designer furniture and accessories. I complimented her on every room that I entered.

"So, who lives here with you?"

"You now and Meeka."

"I want to thank you for all that you are doing. I've never had anyone stick their neck out for me. No one ever showed me that they cared about me."

"It's no problem. I care about all of the girls that I work with, and I do my best to keep a family-oriented atmosphere. You'll see that we are all so close and my girls never want to leave. Some of them have been working with me since the day I started this business. Any of them will tell you that working for me was the best decision that they ever made. They could have all gone to college, but they would have never been making the profits that they make now. But I don't want to bore you with all of this family talk because we have things to do. I'm going to take you to my hairdresser and get your hair done. Then we'll get your nails and feet done. You're going to be the perfect promoter," she said, as she smiled.

"OK," I said, returning a smile.

I was happier than I had ever been in my life at that point. Dyna's stylist Ariana cut my hair into a wrap with long, feathered layers. She also gave me some blonde highlights and I loved it. The hairstyle made my face look drastically different. After getting my nails and feet done, we went back to the store. It was now 8:00PM, and I soon saw the process of the escort business. The dates were pre-arranged by Dyna and paid for in advance. There were drivers who doubled as security for the escorts. The type of car depended on the client. Sometimes it would be a small car or other times a limo. The hotel rooms were paid for in advance as well, and the drivers drove the women to the locations where they would meet there dates or "tricks." The escorts would then perform what-ever sexual activity the man wanted. The rates were by the hour, and the man would pay for as many hours as he wanted the escort to stay. The hourly rate went anywhere from $300 to $1000 depending on your reputation and experience. It also depended on the amount of time the client wanted with them. Some overnight or out of town trips made the rate go up. The new girls always started with $300 and moved their way up. You could also be re-duced on hourly pay if Dyna was pissed at you.

This was a crazy business, one I was glad I would only be promoting and not directly involved in. After Dyna gave all of the girls their directions, she sat and counted all of her money for the night and also separated each girl's pay, placing their money into envelopes labeled with their names on them. I looked at Dyna as a goddess. A woman with that much power was something I had never wit-nessed before, and I felt privileged to even know her.

After closing up her store, we went back to her house for the night. After showering and changing into my PJ's, I told Dyna that I would be going to bed.

"Well good-night! I've had a long day and I want to rest up so that I can do my best tomorrow on my first day of work," I said, smiling.

"I'm glad that you're on my team now. I just want you to know that. I feel good about you, and I feel like we are going to be really good friends in the future. I feel like I can trust you, and I hope everything that I feel is true."

"It's definitely true. I appreciate everything you are doing for me, and I would never do anything to ruin that. I've never had anyone in my life who cared about me, and for that reason I will always be loyal to you."

"I'm very happy to hear that. So go ahead and rest up. Give me hug!" she said, reaching out to hug me.

As soon as she hugged me, Meeka came into the room and again gave me the evil eye. I quickly loosened my grip and greeted her. She just waved. I told them both good-night and made my way to the bedroom which would now be mine. No longer did I have to share a room with my careless sister.

I had a very hard time sleeping the first night at Dyna's. The bed was comfortable and the room was perfect, but I just wasn't used to things being perfect. I got up and decided to go to the kitchen to get a glass of water. Moving through the dark hallway, I noticed a streak of light coming from Dyna's room. I walked up to the door which was cracked and noticed Dyna naked appearing to be engaged in some sexual act. Moving a little closer to the door, I could then see Meeka down on her knees pleasing Dyna with strokes of her tongue. I had never seen two women engaging in sex before, but it was amazing. I could hear Dyna moaning as she rubbed her hands across her breasts.

"Yes, right there!" Dyna continued to moan.

Meeka soon began using her fingers as well. Watching them gave me a tingle down below that I had never experienced before. Meeka stood up, appearing to be wearing a dildo strapped around her waist. She turned Dyna over, entering her from behind and making her moans of ecstasy even louder.

"Fuck me harder! Meeka, yes, just like that!" Dyna screamed as Meeka rammed the dildo deep inside of her. I stood there quietly watching the entire act, which lasted about 35 minutes. When I realized that they were done, I quickly moved away from the door into the kitchen, hoping they never realized my presence. I sat in the kitchen and prayed that neither of them would notice that I was even awake. I was relieved when I noticed the bedroom light go out. I snuck back down the hallway into the guest room, climbed into the bed, and went back to sleep.

The next morning I woke up to the bright light of the sun shining in through the wooden mini blinds. I looked over at the clock and noticed that it was 9:00 AM. I got up and brushed my teeth before going out of the room to see what Dyna had planned for the day. Going downstairs to the living room, I found Meeka sitting on the sofa watching TV.

"Good morning!" I said.

"What's so damn good about it?"

"I'm alive, you're alive, that's what's good," I replied cheerfully.

"Whatever, little girl. I hope you enjoyed the show last night. I saw you standing out in the hall watching us. Dyna did that shit purposely because she likes an audience. "

"What are you talking about?" I said bashfully.

"You know what I'm talking about, and to set the record straight right now, Dyna is mine! Don't you forget that shit. The fact that you watched is enough, and that should have been enough to get rid of your curiosity. If I ever hear about you even smelling her pussy, your ass will regret it. Do we have an understanding?"

"I'm not gay, Meeka, so you don't have to worry about that."

"I wasn't gay when I met her either! All I have to say is that you better keep your hands off of her."

"Well I already told you that I'm not gay. Hell, I'm still a virgin. I'm not trying to start any trouble. I just want to save my money to put myself through college."

"Well, don't think that we are ever going to be friends. I don't trust you. Truthfully I don't trust anyone. You just need to stay out of my way."

"I will, that's not a problem," I said before walking away.

I was angry that she would say those things to me. It had never crossed my mind to get with Dyna sexually. She was very pretty indeed, but I didn't understand where Meeka's animosity was coming from. I went back to the bedroom and picked out an outfit to wear. I chose a denim mini, a pink beaded tank, and pink pumps. I fixed my hair in a ponytail and applied some lip-gloss to make my lips pop. Shortly after I was dressed, Dyna came into the room.

"Good morning!" she said, smiling.

"Good morning," I replied.

"So are you ready for work? You look good in that mini, girl. I wish I had an ass like that. They'd be calling me unstoppable!" she laughed.

Bashfully I replied, "Yes I'm ready."

"Well, I'm going to send you down to the neighborhoods where the top hustlers hang at and you can just go and give out flyers and use your looks to get their attention."

"What do you mean use my looks?"

"You're fine, girl! You have to use that to your advantage. Make them come to you and when they do, sell the business."

"I hope I don't punk out."

"Trust me, you won't. There will be $1,000 waiting for you at the end of the day."

"Are you serious?" I already thought that she had given me too much, but $1000 definitely seemed a little extreme.

"Very serious. I figure $1,000 a day is good. You'll be out on your feet all day, so I hope that those pumps are comfortable. Do you know how to drive?"

"No."

"Well I'm going to have to teach you, because I can't afford to have someone driving you around. I need everyone to do their own driving. But for now I'll put you out with Jenna. You and her can go to the different spots together until I can teach you how to drive."

"OK."

After introducing me to Jenna, we drove around until we reached the first spot that we would go to work at. It was a bar where she said a lot of the big time hustlers hung out. Jenna was a Puerto Rican girl with long, black hair with blonde highlights placed throughout. She looked to be about a size 2. She really didn't have much of a shape, but she did have a gorgeous face. I felt close to her even though we had just met. Our conversation was good, and our chemistry was great. I knew we would make a great team.

We got out of the car and entered the bar. I instantly became nervous when the men began calling us in every direction. Jenna told me not to be nervous, but that was very hard to do because I had never received that type of attention from men before. One man called me over to him, and I didn't hesitate to go over. He was fine with smooth skin the color of coffee with extra cream. His teeth were perfect, and I could smell his cologne a mile away. I was interested to know more about him even though I was supposed to be promoting the business. I smiled and put on a switch courtesy of my Baby Phat pumps.

"What's up?" I said, in a sexy tone.

"You, ma! That's for damn sure."

"Have you ever heard of Dymes Clothing?"

"Clothing?" He began laughing. "I've heard of Dymes, but it definitely ain't have nothing to do with clothing. Shit, if that's where you work. I'll spend all my money for a night with you."

"No, I don't work the field; I just promote it. If you know about the business, then I'm sure you know about the girls."

"Yeah, but I'm not interested in them. I'm interested in you."

"Well, I'm working now, so I can't really help you now."

"Well, let's make a deal."

"Deal? Why should I make a deal with you?"

"Look, I promise to send that business ten customers with your name as a referral if you let me take you out on a date. I know that your boss will appreciate that."

"I don't know. I would have to think about that."

"What is there to think about? I know you want to. It's no reason to be scared."

"Do you promise to send the customers?"

"I told you that already. I keep all of my promises."

"Well, give me your number, and after I hear that you sent the customers, I'll call you."

"That's a deal, baby. My name is JT and here's my business card. I'm a party promoter as you can see. What's your name, ma?"

"Sugar."

"Really? I like that! I look forward to hearing from you soon, Ms. Sugar. I hope you're that sweet!" He laughed.

"No problem. You scratch my back, and I'll grant your wish!" I smiled before walking away. I moved around the bar, going from hustler to hustler and telling each of them about the business. I could feel JT's eyes burning a hole in my back with each step I took. I knew it would be hard not to call him because for a change a guy wanted me, and it excited me to the tenth power. We worked that bar for about an hour before leaving to hit the next spot. Each place was basically the same. All I could think about was JT, and though many other guys tried to spit game that day, their words had no effect on me. JT was the winner that day, and if he could keep his promise, it would be my pleasure to go out on a date with him.

After a long day of work my feet were killing me. As soon as we reached Dyna's office, I took my shoes off and rubbed my tired feet. After she spoke with Jenna and paid her, I gave Jenna a hug before she left. I was happy about how the day had gone, and yet I was nervous that Dyna wouldn't be satisfied with my work. Instead, she was ecstatic.

"I am so happy that I hired you, Sugar. You did a really good job today! I have never had a girl do so well on her first night of work. You'll be happy to know that fifteen customers called here today and booked escorts with your name as a referral."

"Are you serious?"

"I can't believe it myself. Some of the other girls didn't get that many in a week!"

"Wow, that's great, Dyna."

"It is, and for that, you're getting an extra $500 on your pay. Keep up the good work," she said, passing me the envelope containing $1,500.

"So, do you have any plans tonight? You should go out and celebrate."

"I don't have any plans yet, but I am definitely going to celebrate!" I laughed.

"Well, I'll have one of the drivers take you to home."

"OK, thanks so much, Dyna."

"Here's a cell phone too. The number is on the back. It's yours to keep until you want to get one of your own, but that's the business phone, OK?"

"OK!" I gave her a hug and went downstairs to wait on the driver. I took the business card out of my pocket that read Game Recognize Game ENT. I flipped the card through my fingers, whispering his name over and over again. Once the driver pulled up, I got inside and dialed the number.

"Hello!" a deep voice spoke.

"Hi, is JT available?"

"Speaking, who is this?"

"Sugar."

"Oh, I guess you got my referrals, huh?"

"Yeah, I did and I appreciate it a lot. You got me a bonus for that."

"That's good. So are we going out tonight or what?"

"Sure, where do you want to go?"

"Let that be a surprise. Where do you want me to pick you up from?"

"I can meet you somewhere."

"OK, well meet me at the bar where I met you at 11:00PM."

"OK, cool." I called Dyna and asked her if it was OK for the driver to drop me off. She approved and let the driver know to wait on me until I changed. I got in the house and struggled to find something to wear. I ended up with a little black dress that hugged all of my curves. There was a time that I thought that I was overweight, but since meeting Dyna I now appreciated my size 8 frame. I had a round butt that most women would die for and every man wanted to grab. Those were Dyna's words to describe it. After showering and changing, I ran back out to the car and directed the driver to my destination. It wasn't long before we reached the bar.

Nervously I got out of the car to find JT leaning up against a white Expedition. I smiled as I walked in his direction after signaling the driver to leave. I switched over to him with my sexy newfound walk and he grinned from ear to ear, looking me up and down. Once I reached him, we hugged and the smell of his cologne tickled my nose.

"You look good, girl. Damn good!" he said, licking his lips like LL Cool J.

"I'm glad that you approve."

"So let's go," he said, walking me around to the passenger side door.

"I would have worn something different if I'd known I had to climb up in this big truck."

"Sorry, I like big trucks." He smiled.

I climbed into the truck, shortly exposing my black thong; I could see the delight on his face as he peeked. Our night began with dinner and we talked about our lives.

"So how did you get into the business that you're in?"

"I had a big fight with my mom and I had to leave. I had met my boss while working at Bloomingdale's. As a mater of fact, I have to call them and let them know that I won't be coming back."

"You like your job that much huh?"

"I need the money, that's all. What about you, do you like your job?"

"Yeah, I love partying, so to make money while partying, it's a no brainer."

"I bet you get a lot of women falling all over you."

"Not at all, a lot of women are scared of me. They think I'm a playboy."

"So you don't have a woman?" I couldn't believe a man with his looks and smooth talk would actually be single.

"I'm not dedicated to anyone," he replied, staring me in the face.

"So I guess that means that you have friends that you have sex with?" I tried to keep eye contact, hoping I would be able to catch him in a lie. I would hate to gain feelings for him and find out later on that he in fact had a girlfriend.

"I didn't say that," he laughed.

"What's so funny?"

"That you asked me that, I told you that I'm not dedicated to anyone, and that's what's important. What about you?" He quickly turned the heat on to me.

"I've never had a man before. I'm still a virgin."

Laughing hysterically, he said, "Get the fuck out of here! You are out here promoting an escort business and you expect me to believe that you are a virgin? That's some bullshit if I ever heard it."

"I'm serious! Today was my first day, and before that, no guy has even looked my way," I said, defending myself. I knew that I wasn't lying, hell I had no reason to. Though I could understand why he would find what I said humorous, it wasn't funny to me. I hoped that everyone wouldn't assume that I was loose.

"That's really funny, but if you say so I believe you." He smiled. "So what do you want to do when we leave here? Now that you tell me you are a virgin, I'm sure we won't be heading to my spot."

"Who said we couldn't go to your house? Is sex all you want?" I asked, concerned that sex was his only intention from the start.

"Not at all. I want you to be my girl eventually, but sex is definitely part of the plan. That's part of any relationship ain't it?"

"Yeah, I guess it is. So if things work eventually, we'll get to that, but for now we can go to your spot and chill."

"Cool."

After eating we drove to his apartment in Southwest Philly. It was a large two bedroom apartment, much larger than the apartment that I lived in with my family. JT's apartment was definitely all masculine. Black leather furniture, *Scarface* pictures on the walls, a huge fish tank with all different types of exotic fish. Playstation games piled up from the floor almost stood as tall as me. There were random boots and sneakers on the floor in different spots and rooms. It smelled like cologne, which was good. The scent was one that I remembered from the moment I met him.

He turned on the TV as I made my way to the sofa and sat down. The sofa was really comfortable being as though I was not used to nice furniture.

"What's wrong, why do you look like that?" he asked

"Like what?"

"Like you're afraid. Trust me, I don't bite unless you ask me to!" he laughed.

"I'm cool, I'm just taking in my surroundings, that's all."

Sitting on the sofa next to me he said, "You know that after I saw you at the bar earlier, I couldn't get you off my mind. I think that you are going to make me happy."

"So what do you think you are going to do for me?"

"I don't think, I know that I'm going to make you happy. That's my motto, never leave a woman unhappy no matter what. That's how you keep them coming back."

"So, that's how you do it, huh?" I replied sarcastically.

"Look, I'm trying to be serious with you. For real, I want to rip your clothes off right now and fuck you real good, but I know that's not what you want, and I'm a respectable dude. I'm just making small talk to keep my mind occupied."

"Well what if I took my clothes off for you, would that ease your mind? I paid too much money for this dress to have it ripped off," I said in a seductive tone. I don't where I got the heart to give in to temptation, but for some reason I believed him and I wanted to be happy. I trusted what he said, and the fact that I felt so comfortable around him eased my mind. I wasn't afraid to give myself to him and I prayed that it would be well worth it.

"What?" he asked, confused.

I stood up from the sofa and looked at him once more. His pleased expression told me that I couldn't turn back now. I slowly unzipped the side of my dress, and after taking both arms out of the sleeves I let it drop to the floor. I stood there in my bra and thong, watching him squirm in his seat. I don't know where I had got the heart to act in the manner I was, but the adrenaline rush had me stripping like a professional.

After I was completely naked, I walked over to him, sat on his lap, and began kissing him. His lips were soft, and I savored the taste of his tongue as he forced it into my mouth. I began feeling that tingle down below again as he rubbed all over my back in a frenzy. His kisses went from my lips to my neck, which intensified my excitement. Soon he picked me up and carried me to his bedroom, where he placed me on the edge of the king-sized bed. I laid there patiently as he took off all of his clothes in what seemed like a few seconds, only leaving his boxers. His large member protruded through his boxers, now making me afraid of the pain that I was about to experience.

"Are you sure that you want to do this?" he asked, breathing heavily.

Raising up to kiss him, I didn't say a word, and he knew what time it was. He began licking all over my breasts in a circular motion, making me weak. I had never experienced this sort of feeling before, and at that point I wished that I had not waited so long to lose my virginity after all. I wished that JT had come around a long time ago. He moved his tongue down to my stomach, continuing the same motion on my navel. I had butterflies in my stomach as he moved farther downtown. I held my breath, preparing for the next spot that he would reach as he took his tongue and slowly licked my clit, sending me to ecstasy at first contact. I wasn't sure what the feeling was, but my body began to shiver uncontrollably. He giggled a little after noticing my paralyzed state. After pleasuring me a little more, he grabbed a condom, put it on, and whispered in my ear softly, telling me to let him know if I wanted him to stop. I definitely didn't want him to stop because everything thus far had felt so good. My body was yearning for more. I could feel the heat from his body, and I wanted him inside of me. He kissed me passionately as he took his swollen member in his hand and guided it toward my love nest.

At first the pain was excruciating, but I held in my screams, hoping that it would get better with every stroke. I was fooled. Though it was a little better every time, it still hurt like hell. It seemed like eternity before JT moaned in fulfillment, he then went down and kissed my swollen lips as they throbbed and ached from the pounding that they had received. I laid there unsure of what to say as JT laid beside me and placed his muscular arm across my body. I felt secure, and I had no regrets and that was a good thing because I couldn't change what happened. What's done is done.

"Are you OK with what just happened?" he asked with concern.

"Yeah, I'm fine. Why did you ask that?"

"I just wanted to make sure I didn't hurt you too bad. I know I'm working with some major weight down there!" he said, laughing.

"So are you going to kick me out now, or am I staying the night?"

"I'm not cold like that, ma. I wouldn't do that. I want to lay next to you tonight, and I want to see your face when I wake up in the morning if that's cool with you."

"That's perfect," I said, smiling before kissing him.

We fell asleep in each other's arms that night and it was better than I could have dreamed. I never imagined that my first time would be that way. I didn't want to wake up if it was dream; I wanted to be happy for once because I felt I deserved it. I didn't have any experience with relationships, but I was willing to learn and be the best woman that I could be.

The following morning, I woke up and showered before JT dropped me off at work. Luckily I had an extra outfit at the store because I didn't have enough time to go back to Dyna's and change. I kissed JT goodbye before getting out and running in the store and up the stairs to Dyna's office. She was just finishing up a phone call when I walked in.

"I see you had an all nighter! I hope you enjoyed yourself. Who was the lucky guy?" she asked.

"A guy I met named JT and I did enjoy myself, thanks."

"JT, huh? Well good for you. Just don't get too wrapped up with these men. It's bad for business. Jenna's going to pick you up out front for work. Bring me some more ballers, OK?"

"OK," I said, before leaving the office.

I changed and then went down and waited for Jenna to arrive. I daydreamed as I thought about the previous night's events. I felt like a woman now, no longer a little girl hiding behind my virginity. I continued to work as a promoter during the day and spent my nights with JT over the next six months. I was always happy when we were together, and I told him that every chance I got. Though I hated him going out partying so much, I knew that it was his job. He hated my job too, but he dealt with it because he wanted to be with me. It was only right that I did the same. **What's good for the goose is good for the gander!**

Chapter 3

Dollar Signs

JT was promoting a party for a rapper from Philly named Top Dollar. He had been spreading the word for months in advance. His phone was constantly ringing off the hook with people wanting to know how they could attend. It was a private party, so only the people that they invited would get in. I had never heard of Top Dollar before because I didn't listen to rap music. I was more into smooth R&B; I didn't care to hear about people getting killed, drugs, and money in every song. JT asked me to attend the party as I did most of his parties. I had shopped all morning for the perfect outfit and when I did find it, I was so excited. I wanted all eyes to be on me, and I wanted my man to be proud of what he had. I was the bomb, no doubt!

Jenna decided to go to the party with me since she was pissed at her boyfriend. They had been mad at each other for days, so she thought that going to this party would make him even more upset. My relationship with JT had blossomed so much in the past six months. I was turning into wifey, a role that I was happy to accept. Though I can admit that I was losing focus on school, in the back of my mind I knew that I would go eventually. I was having fun now—enjoying the new people, clothes, money—everything was too good to leave behind at that point.

When we reached the party it was packed. I had never seen so many people in a club at once. I was sure that if the police knew about the abundance of people they would shut it down for sure. The music was loud and the club was dark. I searched for JT until I found him in the lounge talking with a group of guys.

"Hey, baby!" I said, kissing him.

"Fellas, this is my girl Sugar. Sugar, this is Top Dollar and his crew."

"Hello," I said, astonished by the beauty in front of me.

"I'm talking business right now, so I'll find you in a little bit, OK?"

"OK. I'm here with Jenna so I'll be cool," I said before walking away.

I couldn't help but think about the man that I had just seen. Though my man was fine, Top Dollar was that to the tenth power. I was mesmerized by his style; his diamond filled chain and dollar sign pendant hypnotized me. I couldn't imagine the value of his jewelry. His hair was nicely braided and his mustache was perfectly trimmed. His teeth sparkled even in the dim club lighting. I was far from a groupie chick; I had a man, a good one at that but it was OK to have dreams. I went out on the dance floor as Jenna followed. We danced for about five songs straight before heading back to the bar to get a drink. I sat on the stool and placed the order while Jenna went to use the rest room.

"So you love your man, huh?" a deep toned voice spoke in my ear.

I turned around and found Top Dollar standing behind me. "Yes I do."

"That's good, but I saw how you looked at me, and you can holla at me and still love your man."

Shocked I asked, "What?"

"I'm going to give you my card. Holla at me when you want a nigga that really knows how to work the middle. I know that nigga ain't hitting it right or you wouldn't have been looking at me like that."

"Looking at you like what?"

"Like you want to get fucked."

"Really, I wasn't aware that there was a look for that."

"You know what look I'm talking about, and we both know what you want."

"Isn't JT your friend?"

"I don't have friends. He's a business associate. Look just hit me when you're ready," he said slyly before passing me the business card and disappearing into the crowd of the club.

What the hell was that about? I thought. Though Top Dollar was fine, I would never take it as far as to have sex with him. He was crazy as hell if he thought I would mess up my relationship with a good man for a quick screw. I laughed to myself as I placed the business card on the bar. Soon Top Dollar was performing the last song of the night and we danced to the music, Jenna and I both rather tipsy from the Alize and Hennessy mix called "Thug Passion" that we had been drinking. Dyna had provided me with a fake ID, so I was able to drink and get into the clubs with no problem. I watched him on stage and he looked even better in the light. I shook myself back to reality when JT came behind me and wrapped his arms around my waist.

"Hey baby, you ready to go?" he asked, smiling.

"Sure, we just have to walk Jenna to her car."

"No problem."

After JT said all of his goodbyes we walked Jenna to her car and began our drive home. I had to find a way to question JT about Top Dollar without seeming like a groupie; I wanted to know more about him.

"So, how long have you known Top Dollar?"

"Oh, we go way back. I've known him since middle school."

"He seems nice. What part of Philly is he from?"

"Germantown, and what's with all the questions about him?"

"Nothing, I'm just making conversation, baby."

"Well I don't want to talk about another nigga."

"OK, sorry."

With that I ended the conversation. Top Dollar had to be put out of my mind—for now anyway. Once we reached the apartment we began foreplay immediately. The alcohol that I had been drinking intensified my sexual feelings.

For the past six months I had been having sex with JT almost every night with the exception of that time of the month and the nights that he didn't come home. During this time I had been mostly staying at his house. Dyna wasn't too happy about it, but allowed it as long as I reported to work on time and still performed the job as I did before JT.

I had become something like a professional, and JT loved every minute of it. I had learned how to work him in every position, even bouncing my booty back at him when he hit it from the behind. Sex had evolved into something that I had enjoyed; far different from the first time we had sex. We fell to sleep, both exhausted, shortly after our one-hour sexual escapade. The next morning JT dropped me off at work as usual, and Jenna and I made our way out to the streets.

"Girl, what was up with that nigga Dollar? He was all on you last night."

"I don't know. He was fine as hell, though. I tried to ignore his ass, but the way he was talking to me made my panties wet, girl!" I laughed.

"You better keep that shit to yourself. You know JT will kill you if you fuck around on him."

"No, I wouldn't do that. But I can dream about it, though." I smiled.

"Shit! That nigga is paid, I would fuck him," she said, laughing.

We continued our workday as usual. I was beginning to like my job because the money was much more than I was used too. I was still planning on moving out of Dyna's to get away from Meeka. Meeka felt threatened by my relationship with Dyna. We had become close and that put a strain on their relationship. I knew that the longer I stayed there, the more likely Meeka and I would come to blows. I was still saving my money for college, though I hadn't saved as much as I should have because I would randomly splurge on clothing for work.

We decided to stop by a few bars up and down Broad Street; we usually hit the bars off small streets but decided to do things differently, hoping to score some big money. While making rounds in one bar I heard a male voice call my name. I looked around until I saw where the voice was coming from. Shocked, I saw Top Dollar sitting in the back of the bar with a cigarette in his hand. I was nervous as I walked over to where he was sitting.

"You didn't call me!" he said, blowing smoke out of his mouth.

"I know, I never told you that I would."

"I know you wanted to. I don't know why you are playing hard to get. I know your type, and I know that you can't resist me."

"What do you mean 'my type'? I am not a groupie chick, and I have money of my own if you think I'm attracted to that!" I was annoyed.

"I'm glad you have your own money, but I have something that you need."

"And what's that?"

"Good dick! I'm just trying to hook you up. Now if you don't want it, then tell me now."

"Listen, the offer is tempting, but I love JT and that's who I'm staying with."

"I'm not asking you to leave him. Sex ain't got nothing to with that."

"Yes it does, because if he finds out he'll leave me for sure."

"He won't find out. I promise you that."

"Just give me your number again and I'll think about it."

"You might as well just say yes now, because that's what you are eventually going to say."

"Look, I have to finish working so I'll call you if that's what I decide."

"Cool!" he said, passing me another business card. The business card didn't even have a name, just a few dollar signs and a number. I guess that was his way of keeping the groupies from calling if the card was accidentally found. I thought it was silly. Why the hell did he have a business card anyway? I mean, he wasn't a huge name like Jay-Z, but he had the potential to be. If he was smart, he'd lose the business cards.

I knew I shouldn't have even taken the card, but I did think he was fine. I loved JT with all of my heart, so why was I even thinking of sleeping with another man? I placed the card in my wallet and finished working. After work the driver dropped me off at JT's apartment, and he wasn't there. I called his cell phone and left a message when he didn't pick up. Bored, I showered, and after watching TV for a while I fell to sleep on the sofa. I woke up around 10:00 PM, and JT still hadn't come home. I was pissed when I noticed that he hadn't called either. I knew he was probably out with another chick, and that was something that I had grown used to. I knew from the first night that he had friends that he slept with, and even though it bothered me when he was out, he always came home to me. The females occasionally would call the apartment when he wasn't there. There were also many inconsistencies in his whereabouts, but I wanted to believe that I was his number one, even if there was a number two or three on the side. I called him once more, and after still not getting an answer, I pulled the business card from my wallet and called Top Dollar.

"Hello!"

"Hi, is this Dollar?" I asked nervously as I tried to cover it with a sexy tone.

"Yeah. Who is this?"

"Sugar."

"Oh, so you decided to call. What's up?"

"Can you come and pick me up?"

"Pick you up? From where?"

"JT's apartment."

"Are you sure about that?"

"I'm positive; he's out with one of his chicks, so he won't be coming home anytime soon."

"All right, I'll be there in a half."

"OK."

I was nervous as I sat there waiting for him to arrive.

What the hell am I getting myself into? I thought. I had to get some pleasure, and if JT wasn't going to do it, then Dollar was the next man in line. I couldn't keep allowing myself to just sit home wasting away while JT was out having fun screwing other chicks. I put on a short denim skirt with no panties; I had just shaved, so there would be no pubic hair in the way of my satisfaction. I had on sandals that tied up my legs, giving a dramatic look to my outfit. Last was a slightly see-through tank with no bra. I wanted Dollar to drool when he saw me. I wanted him to give me something that I would never forget, and I wanted this act of betrayal to be well worth it.

Once he beeped the horn, I ran out of the house and entered on the passenger side. He told me how nice my outfit was as I got in. We really didn't talk much on the ride to his apartment, nor did we talk much when we got there. Upon entering his house he immediately started kissing and fondling me. I was excited and he became even more excited when he noticed that I was panty-less. Soon he dropped his pants and boxers to the floor, picked me up, and placed my back against the wall before ramming his large member deep inside of me. With my skirt around my waist, my butt was pressed firmly against the wall as he pounded me harder and harder. This rough sex was something different, but I loved it. I screamed his name over and over again as my juices flowed out of me and down his legs. After turning me in every position imaginable, he exploded all over my behind and though I felt guilty, I was satisfied. I felt that it was worth it because JT had never given it to me like that before. This wouldn't be the last time that Dollar and I would be one and over the next two months. Every time he was in town he would call me and we would meet up.

I tried my best to get JT to spend more time with me,

but each time I failed. I would go out and buy one of the sexiest lingerie sets and cook a full meal and wait for him to come home only to end up disappointed when he wouldn't show up. It was the beginning of the week, and I had only seen JT in passing over the weekend. I called him to find out if would be coming home that evening.

"Hello."

"Hey, baby. I just wanted to know if you were coming home tonight. I have something special planned."

"Something special like what?" he rudely responded.

"It's a surprise, if I tell you it will ruin everything."

"Well I'll be there by eleven," he replied.

"OK, baby. Please don't stand me up," I pleaded. I really wanted us to spend time together since we had been missing out on it lately.

"I'll be there."

I planned to perform for him that night, hoping that he would see what he had been missing out on the past few months. I was ready and sitting on the sofa at eleven waiting for him to arrive. I became anxious at 11:30 and angry by 12:00. I was furious by the time he stumbled in at 1:00 drunk. I was still sitting in the living room when he walked in.

"I'm sorry, babe. I tried to be here."

"You didn't try hard enough," I sharply responded. I was angry that he didn't even put forth the effort to be there on time. Even after I told him how special the night would be.

"I got caught up at work."

"At a party! You are pissy drunk! I guess it's not important for you to spend time with me anymore," I yelled as I stood up from the sofa.

"It is important. I said I tried, but I got caught up. I'm here now, so what's the problem?"

"I'm angry now, that's the problem! I had a whole night planned for us, and you stood me up the same as you usually do. I'm tired of that shit, JT!" I began to walk toward the bedroom because I didn't even want to see his face at that point.

"Well I'm tired of arguing with you every time I come in this muthafucker, but that doesn't stop you from tripping on me!" he yelled, walking in my direction.

"I don't want to argue, I just want to spend time with you."

"Well you just wasted my time with this bullshit! Look I'm out. I'll talk to you later," he spat before walking toward the door.

"JT, wait!" I pleaded. "Look I'm sorry, OK? Could you please just stay with me tonight?"

"How sorry are you?" he asked, with his back still facing me.

"Baby, it won't happen again, so please just come over here."

He turned and looked at me with a slight smile. I knew that I had reeled him in when he started walking toward me. Though I was still angry, I refused to let him walk out on me and go spend the night with someone else. Once he reached the spot where I was standing, he stared at me before pulling me close and kissing me on my neck. The warmth of his breath against my neck sent chills through my body. I became wetter with each flicker of his tongue. As moans escaped with deep breaths, JT untied my robe to reveal my lingerie. His hands rubbing against the small of my back made me more excited. It had been weeks since we'd had sex, and I was looking forward to feeling his hardness deep inside of me.

He prolonged the foreplay by laying me down and kissing and sucking on my nipples, which were already standing at attention. I continued to imagine him inside of me as he played with my wetness. His fingers moving in and out of me felt better than ever before. I moved my hips as he continued to make love to me with his two fingers.

"JT, please fuck me, I need to feel you," I begged.

"How bad do you want it?"

"I want you bad, baby. I need you. Make love to me," I pleaded.

"Do you love me?"

"Yes, I love you," I moaned before he removed his fingers and went down and began to kiss me down below and suck the juices from me. Though his tongue action was excellent, I wanted him inside of me, and I continued to beg him for more. He moved up to kiss me one last time before slowly beginning his stroke. The steady circles that he made inside of me were smooth and easily caused me to orgasm. We switched to different positions often, and each one felt better than the one before. I screamed his name as he matched my orgasm and reached his peak.

Soon after we were done JT took a shower and got dressed. He waved goodbye to me before leaving. Though I was pissed that he was leaving again, I had my fix for the night and I was able to fall asleep satisfied.

I felt like a one-night stand following that night. JT fell right back in line with his disappearing act. I should have known that things wouldn't change. I got a phone call from Jenna letting me know that Dollar was coming to town over the weekend. I went out to buy an outfit to go to the party. Jenna agreed to go with me to the party and JT was out of town so I knew he wouldn't be there to get in the way of me getting close to Dollar once more.

Saturday couldn't come fast enough and I was dressed almost two hours early excited about going to the club. I was dressed in an all black dress that accentuated every curve. The niggas would be drooling when I walked through the club. Once we arrived I wasn't surprised by how packed the small club was. I instantly began searching the room, and when I didn't notice him anywhere, I decided to go to the bar and have a drink. After ordering I pulled Jenna out to the floor to dance. I was feeling a buzz soon after I gulped two shots of Hennessey. We danced for three songs straight when I felt a tap on my shoulder. I turned around to find Dollar's fine ass standing behind me.

"I knew you would come," he spoke with confidence.

"How did you know that?"

"Because you can't resist me," he said, moving closer to me.

"So confident, you are. I like that."

"I know you do. I still have to mingle, but after this is over, I can come scoop you and hit you off. If you know what I mean." He laughed before hugging me.

"Who said that I wanted you to hit me off?"

"You wouldn't have come here if you didn't. I know your man's out of town, so make sure you call me, all right?"

"I'll think about it," I said

"Well, don't spend too much time thinking about it. It's a lot of women that would love to take your place for the night."

"I'll keep that in mind."

"Cool," he said before turning and heading in the opposite direction.

I turned to Jenna, who was now dancing with some tall, slim guy. She smiled and gave me thumbs up as I started to sway to the music. Soon, Dollar was onstage performing and the women were going crazy. I looked around at the astonishment on their faces and I felt good. I was glad that I had the opportunity to be with him tonight and enjoy something that all of those women would fight for. Once the party was over I drove Jenna home and she couldn't wait to quiz me about my plans for the night.

"So are you going to hook up with Dollar tonight?"

"I'm not sure. I'm still a little undecided."

"Girl, please. You better get your ass over there and fuck that nigga tonight. You might not get another opportunity after this. JT ain't doing what he's supposed to, so you shouldn't feel the least bit guilty."

"I know, but I told him I would think about it."

"What is there to think about? You need some dick, so go and get it!" she laughed. "I don't want to hear no complaining tomorrow if you go home and play with yourself tonight."

"Whatever! I'll call you in the morning."

"OK," she said, before giving me a hug.

I called Dollar as soon as I was around the corner. I didn't want Jenna to see exactly how anxious I was. He answered the phone on the second ring, and I sat speechless for a second.

"Hello?"

Silence . . .

"Hello!" he yelled.

"Hey Dollar, it's Sugar."

"I guess you realized you wanted me, huh?"

"I already knew I wanted you; I just didn't want to seem like a groupie."

"Well, ain't like we ain't never been together."

"Yeah, that's true."

"Well, are you ready for me to come and get you?"

"Yeah, I'm ready."

"All right, I'll be there in about an hour. Keep it hot for me, all right?"

"I will."

I drove home and jumped in the shower. I was pacing the floor as I waited for Dollar to come and pick me up. It was a few minutes before 4:00 AM when he knocked on the door.

"You on time, I love that," I spoke in a seducing tone.

"You want to be daring?"

"Yeah, I'm up for some excitement."

"Let's go on the balcony."

"Here?" I asked.

"Yeah, here."

"All right," I said, nervously knowing that a lot of JT's friends lived our apartment building.

"Strip!"

I obeyed, removing each article of clothing while walking to the balcony. Once outside, I turned around to find him naked and was instantly aroused. He began stroking his length while motioning me to go down on him. I was a little hesitant at first since he wasn't my man, but I gave in and squatted down in front of him and began to work my magic. He put his hand on the back of my head and guided me as I took his length deep into my mouth. Soon he pulled away and bent me over the gate. I placed one leg on the patio chair as he started to ram me from behind. The night air was turning me on, plus the sounds of people outside excited me even more.

I moaned loudly as he palmed my breast and continued to hit me from the back. His strokes became more forceful as he neared his peak. As he was ready to explode, he pulled out turned me around and released all over me. I was so tipsy that the degrading act didn't even bother me.

I wanted more, and I made sure that I got it before he left me for the night. I fell to sleep that night with a smile on my face. He filled the void that was left from JT's continued disregard of my feelings. I needed sex as well as attention, and Dollar knew how to make me feel wanted.

Things only got worse between JT and me. We had grown more distant from each other. Now that I had Dollar in my life to hit me off, I didn't really care if JT wanted to spend time with me or not. It was a Friday and Dollar wanted to take me to a private party with him and I happily obliged. I put on my best and was excited when we walked into the crowded party. Dollar walked around the club, greeting everyone as I made my way to the ladies' room. I checked my make-up and hair to make sure that it was perfect. After passing inspection, I left the ladies room and was stunned when JT was at the door waiting.

"What the fuck are you doing here with that nigga Dollar like you are his girl or some shit?"

"Excuse me?"

"Excuse me my ass! I had some suspicions that you were fucking him, now I know!"

"JT now is not the place for this shit."

"I knew that I shouldn't have trusted you."

"Fuck you, JT! All of the bitches that you fucked and you are going to blame me."

"You knew how I was from the door. At least I didn't try to front like you did. You got niggas laughing at me because I'm telling them you're my girl and you are out here fucking this dude."

"JT, we need to talk about this later," I said, turning my back to him.

"We are going to talk about this shit now!" he yelled, grabbing my arm.

"Get the fuck off of me, JT."

"I can't stand trifling-ass bitches like you. I should have sent you home after I fucked you the first night. Your pussy ain't never been good anyway!" he spat before walking in Dollar's direction.

I ran over there and noticed JT shaking Dollar's hand with a brief hug. *What the hell?*

"You are so damn stupid, Sugar. I set your ass up and you took the bait! Do you really think a nigga like Dollar was going to take you seriously? I knew that you couldn't be trusted, and I got him to come on to you to see what you would do. I guess I was right!"

"It wasn't hard to get either. She let a nigga hit it without much hesitation at all," Dollar said, laughing.

"I bet you're embarrassed now, and you should be. If you would have been loyal you wouldn't be standing here looking like a nasty-ass ho right now!" JT yelled.

I stood there frozen, and I was so angry that I couldn't even cry. As I looked around the club, I noticed that people were watching and laughing. I couldn't believe that I was the joke of the night. I wasn't going to allow myself to be embarrassed any further. I walked away without saying a word. *Fuck them both!* I felt like the biggest asshole on the planet for getting played like that. Here I thought that I was playing him and he was playing me the whole time. I began to cry as I took off my shoes to walk home. After walking ten blocks I called Dyna to come pick me up. I cried on her shoulder that night, and I was glad that she was my friend. It was times like these that they say make you stronger, but I felt like I couldn't trust another man now. JT had ruined the perfect picture I had of him, and all men for that matter. I knew I had myself to blame for falling for Dollar. I was a fool to think his feelings were genuine. I would never let another man hurt me again. I would never be the laughing stock of anyone's joke again either. Everything happens for a reason, and it was best for me to move on. I never returned to JT's apartment to gather my belongings. I figured he'd probably tossed them anyway. It's a shame how I was blinded by the *dollar signs*. Niggas ain't shit!

Chapter 4

Sisterly Love . . .

I had recently heard through the grapevine that my sister Mya was pregnant again. I wasn't surprised at all because of the lifestyle she lived. I hadn't really talked to her much since the day I left the house. I felt a lot of resentment toward her because of all of the abuse I received. I did have a lot of love in my heart for her, but I hated her at the same time. I was there for her when my niece Jessica passed away due to many birth defects. The cause of the defects was unknown, but it took a toll on her, and my father as well. My mother acted as if she didn't really care; she felt that Mya didn't need a child anyway. I knew that it wouldn't be long before she would get pregnant again, and I was right.

The loss of her daughter calmed her down some. She wanted a family with Marlo and thought that she needed a baby to make things work with him. I thought that your self esteem would have to be extremely low to believe that a baby will make a man stay, but I was sure her conceited act was just a façade. My mother ruinèd my self-esteem, so I knew Mya would have some issues as well.

Though I didn't get to spend much time with Jessica, I did love her. A baby makes you fall in love with them instantly. Jessica was beautiful. She was born premature, and even with all of the tubes and tape all over her tiny face, you could see her smile. Mya was detached during the time the baby was in the hospital. She only lived eight days.

After the incident with Dollar and JT, I put men off for a while; I needed time to enjoy myself. I needed time to be free of a man and not have to worry about rushing home to please anyone. Dyna's birthday was coming, and she decided to have a few people over to celebrate. It wasn't much of a party—just sitting around eating and drinking. The guest list mostly included her employees and her big spending customers. Though I felt a little out of place, I tried my best to enjoy myself. Meeka was drinking heavily at the party, and I could foresee an altercation before the night was over. I sat down next to Dyna to talk once I noticed that she was becoming annoyed with Meeka's over-the-top behavior.

"Hey, are you enjoying yourself?" I asked, tapping her leg.

"It's cool, how about you?" Dyna asked, barely smiling.

"Are you OK" I asked, concerned.

"I'm just a little annoyed, that's all."

"With Meeka?" I asked.

"Yeah, can't you tell? She always acts like that when she gets drunk, falling all over niggas and shit. I'm supposed to be her woman and that's the thanks I get when a nigga with a hard dick comes around! I'm just tired of that shit, Sugar."

"I'm sure, but it's your birthday, Dyna, and you can't let her ruin it."

"I know, but look at her. It's ridiculous!"

"Well, let's go dance and get your mind off of her."

"No, I'm cool right here."

"Come on!" I said, grabbing her by the hand and pulling her out of her seat to dance. It wasn't far into the first song before Meeka interrupted us.

"What the fuck is this? I told you she was off limits!" she yelled.

"Meeka, you are drunk and you need to chill out. I'm just trying to help her enjoy her birthday since you weren't interested."

"What?" she yelled.

"Meeka, please just drop it!" Dyna said.

"Fuck that, this bitch is disrespecting me," she said, pushing me.

"I don't want to fight you Meeka," I said.

"Meeka, back off!" Dyna yelled. "You weren't too worried about me earlier. Why do you care now?" she asked.

"Dyna, that's not true!"

"You always do that shit when you get drunk!" Dyna yelled. "Why don't you just go to your mom's tonight and get sober? We'll talk tomorrow."

"Dyna, please. I'm sorry, baby."

"I said we'll talk tomorrow," Dyna yelled before heading to her bedroom.

"This ain't over, bitch!" she sneered at me before grabbing her bag and walking toward the door. If looks could kill, I would have been dead. The party guests figured that was the cue for them to leave as well. They began to gather their belongings and disperse to their vehicles. I was happy that Meeka left for the night because I was really in no mood to fight.

I was still feeling a buzz from the alcohol that I had been drinking. I went up to the bathroom and began to undress. I bent over to turn on the shower so the water could warm up. As I took off my shoes, I looked at my body in the full-length mirror. I had really developed in the last few years; my breasts were now a full D cup, and my waist was small with round hips and a perfectly rounded butt. I admired how I had changed and I was now secure with my body, especially with all of the attention I had been getting lately. I was no longer embarrassed by what God had given me.

It had been months since a man had touched me, and I was growing hornier and lonelier every day. I sat down on the stool against the wall opposite the mirror. I closed my eyes and placed my right leg up on the side of the tub. I listened to the sound of the shower and imagined it was a rainstorm, and as I could hear the water beating against the glass, I eased my middle finger inside of my tunnel. I caressed my breast with my free hand and continued moving my finger in and out as I moaned loudly. I tickled my clit with my index finger in a circular motion. I could feel the juices pouring out of me as I came three consecutive times. I sat there for a second before I opened my eyes and was stunned to see Dyna standing at the door staring at me. I quickly sat up straight and tried to cover my naked body with my bath towel.

"I'm sorry, Dyna!" I said, shyly.

"What are you sorry for? I enjoyed what I just saw; it made me wet as a matter of fact. Do you mind if I join you?" she asked, moving closer to me.

"I'm not gay, Dyna."

"Neither am I, I'm bisexual. I want to make you feel good, Sugar. No man can give you the feeling that I can," she said, easing down on her knees and placing her hand on my thigh.

"Dyna, please," I said.

"Come on and let me fuck you, Sugar. I've been wanting to since the day I met you," she said as her hands eased up to my lips and began rubbing on my clit. "Ummm, you taste so good!" she said as she licked my juices from her fingers.

"Dyna," I called her name, trying to resist. Her fingers felt so good moving inside of me that I gave in. She continued to move her fingers in and out of me as she sucked on both of my extremely hard nipples.

"Do you want me, Sugar?" she asked as she moved in to kiss me.

"Yes," I moaned.

She moved in the direction to kiss me down below. I could have never imagined that I would be about to have sex with another woman. I had never even been curious about it. Since the first time that I had sex with JT, men were the only thing that I had thought about.

I tried my best to relax as pictures of Meeka kept popping into my head. I remembered her warning, and I prayed that she wouldn't come home and catch us in the motion. I used the tub as leverage to assist me in grinding my clit against her tongue. I continued to moan over and over again. She made love to me with her tongue that night, and it was an experience that I would never forget.

I didn't know what to say to Dyna after it was over. I could barely look her in the eye. It was almost instantly that I began to feel uncomfortable. I had let my loneliness take over, and I knew that I should have gone with my mind on this one. I knew that situation could bring nothing but drama. Meeka was still her girlfriend, and I was still her employee. I was definitely not going to be a jump-off. I felt that I needed to end this before it went any further, and before she went to sleep I went into her room and sat on the edge of the bed.

"Dyna, we need to talk," I said, tapping her on her shoulder.

"What's up?" she said, turning around to face me.

"I really enjoyed myself tonight, but this can't ever happen again."

"Why is that?" she asked before sitting up on the bed.

"Because you are with Meeka and I'm not gay."

"Well, that could change if you want to be with me."

"Dyna, I like you a lot, and I appreciate everything that you've done for me, but I'm not sure I'm ready for that."

"So after what just happened you're telling me that you don't want to enjoy that pleasure all the time?" She moved closer to me.

"I don't know, Dyna."

"Yes you do," she said, moving closer to kiss me.

"I can't, Dyna. I just can't!" I said before getting up and leaving the room. I quickly went to my room and stretched out across the bed. I hoped that Dyna wouldn't take my rejection the wrong way and decide to fire me or put me out. I did want to remain friends minus the lover thing. To be honest, I really did enjoy every minute of the sex. I had never been so satisfied. Dyna pleased me in every way and didn't pressure me to return the favor. I sat there while she feasted on me and it was pure ecstasy. I guess her knowing first hand what makes a woman feel good was where her expertise came from.

It wasn't long before I fell to sleep, and when I woke up to Meeka yelling over top of me, I wasn't sure what the hell was going on. Dyna was standing there in her underwear arguing with Meeka, obviously trying to keep her from attacking me. I rolled out of bed and stood on the opposite side of the bed to move further away from the commotion.

"What's going on?" I asked.

"You know what the fuck is going on! I leave here for one night and when I come home I find you two in the bed together!" Meeka yelled.

"We weren't in bed together!"

"I'm not blind, and I know I walked in here and saw you two 'sleep in the same bed!" She continued to try and get through Dyna and reach me.

"What?" I asked, confused, because I was sure that I went to bed alone last night. She must have climbed into bed with me after I fell asleep.

"Meeka, it's over between us. Me and Sugar are together now!"

"What are you talking about Dyna?" I asked, still unsure of what Dyna was trying to pull.

"I'm going to kill you, bitch!" Meeka yelled.

"Meeka, it's time for you to go. I'll pack your stuff and drop it off to you."

"This shit ain't over," Meeka said. She pushed Dyna out of her way and walked toward the door, continuing to yell obscenities.

"Dyna, why did you lie to her like that?" I asked.

"I didn't lie! We are going to be together and that's final!" she spoke sternly.

"What?"

"I didn't eat your pussy like that just to do it. I did it so you can see what you have to look forward to. I knew you were going to be mine from the day that I met you."

"But Dyna . . ."

"Do you want to go back to your abusive crackhead-ass mother and that fucked up apartment? Because that's the only other option that you have. I'll gladly pack your shit right along with Meeka's things"

"What?" Tears began to well up in my eyes.

"There's no need to cry, Sugar. You'll love being with

me, trust me. I'm going to go get a shower. It would be nice if you joined me," she hinted before leaving the room.

I sat there for a minute in shock. I couldn't believe she would give me an ultimatum like that. I never wanted to go back to my mom under any circumstance, and she knew that. I had nowhere else to go, but I knew that I didn't want to be in a relationship with Dyna. I was so upset that she was going to force me to do something that I had clearly told her I didn't want to do. I didn't have much money saved because she paid me every day, so I didn't waste time spending it. I felt like I was back at home being threatened unless I did everything her way. Dyna had never shown this side to me before.

Within minutes of Dyna leaving the room, I heard the shower running. I knew that I had no other choice but to do what she had ordered me to do. I took off my clothes and nervously made my way to the bathroom. Before going in I took a deep breath and turned my frown into a smile. Though I was burning up inside, I knew that I couldn't let her know it. I walked in just as she was stepping into the shower. She turned around and glanced at me with a devilish grin.

"I'm glad you decided to join me," she said, motioning me to come closer. "I'll guarantee that you will love every minute of what I have to offer."

I didn't say a word as she pulled me into the shower and pushed my back up against the wall. The steam along with the adrenaline had me sweating instantly as she began kissing me on my neck. I closed my eyes and imagined there was a sexy brown-skinned man in the shower with me. I could hear the water beating against her back as she moved down to my stomach and slowly pushed her tongue in and out of my belly button. I began to moan as she moved down lower and placed my leg over her shoulder. She French kissed my lips, and my juices began to flow while she sucked every drop from me. I quickly forgot about the fact that it was Dyna eating me out; the multiple orgasms that she was giving me pushed the idea far into the back of my mind. I wanted her to stop just as much as I wanted her to keep going. My body wanted one thing, but my heart wanted another. It wasn't long before the episode was over, and though I experienced many orgasms, I wanted to go to my room and go to sleep with the hopes that I would wake up and this would all be a dream.

Once I reached my bedroom I slid into bed and lay there staring at the ceiling. What had happened to my life? I questioned all the choices I had made and I wondered if I would have just stayed home and dealt with my mother for a little while longer would I had been better off right now. For some strange reason I missed my mother. Though she abused me for so long, I had gotten used to it, and not having her around was weird. I didn't know what to expect from Dyna. From the day I met her I had built up what I thought she would be in my mind. Once I began working for her she was everything I thought she would be. Sadly, she changed every great thought I had of her. This display of *sisterly love* was something that I would be forced to grow accustomed to.

Chapter 5

Like mother Not Like daughter . . .

I decided to pay my mother a visit since she had been on my mind a lot the last few months. It had been four months since the day I ran out of mother's house. I knew she would probably have nothing nice to say to me, but I still wanted to see how she was doing. After all, she was still my mother and I loved her. I got dressed early on a Saturday in my best gear. I wanted to dress the part to show my mother I had turned out rather well after all she had put me through. Before leaving the house I walked to Dyna's office to let her know where I was going. She was sitting at her desk counting money when I walked in.

"Hey baby! You're all dressed up. Where are you headed to?" she asked, motioning me to come closer so she could get a good look at me.

"To see my mom," I said in a low tone.

"For what?" she asked, shocked.

"Because I haven't seen her since the day that I left, and I want to see how she's doing."

"But why? She never gave a fuck about you, so why do you care about her?"

"Well, unfortunately I'm not like her."

"Yeah, that is unfortunate, because I wouldn't care how the hell she was doing after all that she did to you. She could die and I wouldn't even go to her funeral. Personally, I don't think you should go. But it's your choice, Sugar."

"Well, I'm going to go see her for a few, and I'll come past the store when I'm done."

"All right," she said, kissing me.

I turned to leave the room and I thought about what Dyna had said. You would have to be a cold-hearted person not to attend your mother's funeral. I didn't really know much about Dyna's past, but I could sense that it wasn't great by the things that she said. With all of the things that my mother had said and done to me, I would still attend her funeral because she'd always be the only mother I'd have.

I got into the car that Dyna had bought for me—a new model Toyota Camry. She said that there was more to come, and she was surely making sure that I was happy with what she was giving me. She had even given me a raise in my pay, and I was extremely happy about that. This time I was being a little smarter about saving my money, because I never wanted to be caught out there again broke and forced into an unwanted situation.

Once I reached my mother's apartment complex I sat in the car for a minute. I pondered whether I should go through with it or not. I knew that I had nothing to be afraid of because I didn't depend on her anymore, and I didn't need her to take care of me either. I still had the key to the door, but I decided to knock instead of just walking in. I stood there for about five minutes before my mother stumbled to the door. I could tell that she was high as usual, and she reeked of alcohol. I held my composure and politely said hello.

"What the hell brings you here? Ran out of money?" she said, spitting from the sides of her mouth.

"I just came by to say hi and see how you were doing."

"I don't know why you care about me now," she said, turning around walking inside of the apartment.

"I always cared about you, Mom," I said, following her into the apartment.

"Yeah, right! I heard you're a prostitute now!" she said, grinning.

"No I'm not, Mom. I just promote an escort service, that's all."

"If that's what you want to call it, honey. I ain't no fool, you know."

"That's what it is."

"You're fucking girls now too!"

"Who told you that?" I asked.

"Don't worry about where I get my information from. I know everything."

"Well, if you must know, I am in a relationship with someone, and she treats me very well."

"I know which way you are headed, and it damn sure ain't to nobody's college. I knew you weren't going to be shit!" she spat.

"I am going to go to school, and I hope you're still alive to see it."

"What the hell is that supposed to mean? You think that I'm going to die soon or something?"

"I'm sure you're not going to live very long with all of that heroin you keep shooting into your veins."

"Fuck you, Sugar. If all you came here for was to show off all of your new shit, you can hop off that high horse now, because I don't give a fuck about you or anything you have."

"I'm glad you told me that, Mom. I always had a feeling that you didn't care about me, but now I know for sure. It was nice seeing you anyway," I said, turning to walk out of the apartment.

"Well, the feeling is definitely not mutual," she said, digging the knife even deeper.

I could feel tears welling up as I walked out, but I held them in. I was no longer going to be hurt by anything that she said. I was wiping her out of my life. I now knew that the saying, "like mother like daughter" wasn't always true because I was nothing like her at all. I made my way back out to my car and I noticed Mya walking up the street. I stopped and waited for her to come up to where I was standing.

"What's up, stranger? What brings you around this way?" she asked, smiling.

"I just came by to see how Mom was doing."

"What's been going on? I heard that you're making a lot of money now."

"Not really. It's enough to get by. How have you been doing?"

"I'm cool. You see I'm pregnant again."

"Yeah but, why so soon?" I asked.

"I don't know, it wasn't on purpose. I wasn't going to get an abortion, so I decided to keep it."

"Well, good luck. I hope everything turns out good for you."

"Well, keep in touch. Maybe we can go hang out some time."

"OK," I said before giving her a hug and waving goodbye. I got in my car and watched her as she went into the building. I did hope that everything turned out good for

Mya. After all, she was my sister and I wanted her to be happy.

I drove off with a sense of relief. I finally knew how my mother felt about me, and I could move on. I began driving and my cell phone was ringing in my pocket. I fumbled to answer it without checking the caller ID.

"Hello!" I said.

"What's up, bitch? I hope you didn't think it was over. I'm going to kick your ass when I catch you," Meeka yelled.

"Meeka, I don't know why you continue to call me and harass me. Dyna doesn't want you, and even if she was ever thinking about it, threatening me is not the way to get her back."

"Please, you are just a little pawn in her game. It's a shame that you are too stupid to notice that! She's going to drop you just like she did me when some fresh pussy comes along. You just wait and see."

"Whatever, Meeka. You need to get a life!" I yelled before ending the call. I was furious, and I was sick and tired of arguing with Meeka. At least once a week since the day Dyna put her out she had called and threatened me. She would call me every name in the book just before guaranteeing me an ass-whipping. I had told Dyna on numerous occasions to get Meeka under control, but it didn't appear that she followed through, because Meeka still continued to call me.

I had begun to like this relationship with Dyna over the past few months. Honestly, I had begun to love it. I never thought I could feel that way about another woman. Though Dyna mesmerized me from day one, it had been taken to another level. The way that I felt about her the day I was forced into the relationship had faded away. Her dark-toned skin reminded me of a Tootsie Roll, and she had succulent lips that you just wanted to kiss all the time. Her voice was soft but firm, and her touch was smooth as dark chocolate. With my light brown skin, we were like a candy bar with caramel; we mixed perfectly. I tried not to get upset with Dyna for Meeka's actions, but it was extremely hard. I knew Dyna was capable of taming Meeka if she truly wanted to.

I pulled up in front of the store and parked. I decided to smoke a cigarette before going in to calm my nerves. I had recently picked the. After the scene that had played out at my mother's apartment, I didn't need a repeat from here. I took a couple of puffs before exiting the car and making my way through the store. I greeted everyone on my way to the back to head upstairs. Entering the office, Dyna was sitting at her desk talking with a potential employee. I took a seat on the sofa and waited for her to get done with her interview.

I was becoming impatient as she sat there laughing and giggling. I was becoming angrier with each second as I thought about what Meeka had said to me. I was once the chick sitting there, and now I was where Meeka once was. It was once me sitting there laughing and joking, not sure of what I was getting into while Meeka was sitting there angry that I had even stepped foot in the building. I wanted to interrupt, but I knew that she would flip out. I stared at her while she tried to look away from my direction, avoiding eye contact.

Once she was finished she gave the woman a hug and walked her to the door. It was less than a second after the door shut that I began to speak.

"What the hell was that about?" I asked, placing my hand on my hip.

"What are you talking about, Sugar? That was someone that might work for me in the future."

"Oh, really? What was all of the laughing and shit about? I guess you planning on getting some from her too, huh?" I said, angrily.

"What the fuck is your problem? I guess things didn't go too well at your mom's since you are coming in here tripping for nothing."

"That doesn't have anything to do with it!" I yelled.

"Well then what's your problem?" she asked, sitting back in her office chair.

"You know, I asked you to talk to Meeka, and I assume that you didn't because she continues to call and harass me. I'm tired of that shit, Dyna. You need to do something about that."

"I told you that I would take care of her."

"Well do it then!" I yelled before walking to the door.

"Where are you going?" she asked.

"Home! I'll talk to you later," I said, opening the door.

"Sugar!" she yelled as I left the office and made my way down the stairs.

I was angry, not only at Dyna, but at myself. I had let what Meeka said take me out of my square. I had been doing a pretty good job of dealing with Meeka's comments in the past but after today I knew that I could no longer sit back and take her comments lying down. My cellular phone was ringing as I opened the car door, and I wasn't surprised that it was Dyna. I decided not to answer it. There was nothing left to say at the moment, and I didn't want things to get any worse that they already had.

Driving home, I was still thinking about everything that my mother had said and it sunk in. Maybe I wasn't going to do anything with my life, and maybe I was never going to go to college after all. I was making so much money now that I knew I would make it without college. I did know that I would never turn out like her. I would never turn to drugs to wash my problems away. Once I reached the house, I quickly went to take a shower with the hope that I could get to bed and go to sleep before Dyna came home. Unfortunately, I wasn't that lucky. She was sitting in the bedroom waiting for me to get out.

Entering the room, I noticed the candles lit and smelled the aroma of lilac flowers. I ignored her attempt to rekindle as I dried off and put on my pajamas. Every time we had an argument Dyna would always buy me a gift or try to console me with romance, which would then be followed by make-up sex. Though we didn't really argue that much, I had her routine down to a science. Tonight I was in no mood for sex or romance in any way shape or form.

"Sugar, I'm sorry about today. I promise that I'll talk to Meeka," she said, moving closer to me.

"It's not going to work tonight Dyna. I've had a really long day, and I just want to go to sleep."

"That's cool; I just want you to know that I love you and I'm not going to let anyone come between us. Do you love me, Sugar?"

"Good-night Dyna," I said before climbing into bed. "And yes, I love you too."

I turned over to get comfortable in bed. The truth was that I did love her, even when I was upset. I laid down that night with the hopes that tomorrow would be a better day. It wasn't long before Dyna slid in to bed next to me and wrapped her arms around me. She kissed me on my shoulder and whispered, "I love you," in my ear once more before I drifted off to sleep.

Chapter 6

From Bad to Worse . . .

Things between Dyna and me began to shape up in the three months following our last argument about Meeka. I hadn't been receiving any more phone calls, which was a big relief. Our time together was getting back to normal, and we were enjoying each other even more than before.

Working was beginning to bore me, but I knew I needed to save my money to secure my future. I was tired of being groped by men I wouldn't be caught dead talking to on a non-working day. The fake lines that they would come up with were comical. I would laugh hysterically every night, thinking about the things they would say. Dyna, on the other hand, didn't find it funny. She was always jealous when a man would even look my way. She always thought I would cheat and leave her alone since I had been with men in the past. Even though the feelings I got from men were much different than the feelings I got from Dyna, I didn't have the desire to be with a man. I didn't feel I was ready to be hurt the way that men hurt women. I could never deal with being hurt the way JT hurt me ever again.

I had just left the last bar of the night, and I was exhausted. I went to at least ten bars passing out flyers, and my feet were killing me. I pulled into the gas station after noticing that my gas light was flashing. It was late and the gas station was empty. I used my credit card instead of going inside since my feet wouldn't allow me to walk that far.

A black car pulled in on the opposite site of where I was parked. I glanced at it but turned back around to continue pumping my gas. About five seconds after I heard the cars door open, I was hit on the back of the head with a hard object.

"Help! Help!" I screamed as I stumbled a little while, placing my hand over the spot that was now gushing blood.

I continued calling for help when I noticed that it was Meeka who had hit me from behind. She continued to hit me with what I now noticed was the handle of a gun. I screamed in agony and balled up in the fetal position on the ground as she hit and kicked me. Soon everything went black from all of the pain. I woke up when the paramedic continued to call my name. I could smell the gas that she had obviously poured all over me. My face was throbbing, and my body was numb. The paramedic asked me if there was anyone that he could call, and I gave him Dyna's phone number. Once I reached the ER, the police were there to question me. I was so angry, but I didn't tell them that it was Meeka that did this to me. I knew it would only make things worse. I cried once they left because I could have never imagined that it would go that far. I looked at myself in the mirror on the bedside table and was stunned. My eyes were almost swollen shut, my lips were swollen, and my hair was a wreck. Dyna came in shortly after I was taken to the hospital room where I would be staying in for the next few days.

"Baby, what happened? Who would hurt you like this?" she asked, running over to me and sitting down on the edge of the bed.

"Your crazy-ass ex, that's what's happened," I slowly spoke in anger. Though it was hard for me to speak with my face swollen, I had to let her know how angry I was.

"How do you know that?"

"Because I saw her! How the hell do you think?" I continued to struggle to talk.

"I can't believe that she would do this to you when she knows how I feel about you," she said, placing her hand on top of mine.

Snatching my hand away, I yelled, "Do you think she gives a fuck about that? That bitch tried to kill me! All she cares about is you. I thought you took care of her," I said as tears began to well up in my eyes.

"I thought I did, Sugar. Honestly, you can't believe that I could have predicted this."

"You were with her for over two years. You should have known how crazy she was."

"You can't blame me for this, Sugar. I wouldn't wish anything like this on my worst enemy. It's not my fault that she did this to you."

"Yes it is your fault! You forced me to be with you knowing that she was a crazy, jealous bitch, and now I'm in here after almost being beaten to death all because you can't control her!"

"She has a mind of her own. I can't control her!"

"Bullshit! You can control her; you controlled her while you were with her. The same way you controlled me."

"That's not true."

"You know, I really don't want to have this conversation with you right now. I'm in a lot of pain and I need to get some rest. Is that OK with you? Or is that another thing that you can't do?" I said sarcastically.

"I'm going to let that slide because you're upset right now, and I'm going to leave. You call me when you do want to talk!" she said before getting up to leave the room.

I didn't say anything as she left. I knew that now was the time to distance myself from Dyna since things were getting out of hand. I could no longer deal with this saga that was playing out. I was afraid for my safety, and Meeka definitely wasn't the type to back down. I felt that by not pressing charges on Meeka for the beating and distancing myself from Dyna, Meeka would eventually leave me the hell alone, especially if she thought Dyna and I weren't tight anymore and she could get back in. I didn't ask for any of this, and that's why it hurt so bad. If I had voluntarily gotten myself into this, I would have dealt with it. I felt that I was being betrayed again—the same as I felt with JT. Here I was in love with this chick for whatever reasons, and she couldn't even ensure my safety.

When you enter into a relationship, you want to feel safe and secure, and I felt neither. I felt like she cared about Meeka more than me, and at that point in my life, I wished that she would just get back with her so I could move on. I knew Dyna would never let me go without a fight, and I was in no shape for that. I needed to heal, and I worked on myself for the next three weeks as all of my wounds closed one by one.

I had already decided that I was going to limit the amount of time that I worked. That would give me more free time to myself away from Dyna. The way I figured it, if I hung out without her a lot she would become fed up and eventually move on. I continued, but I didn't hit the streets as much. I had to practically beg Dyna to limit my outings since I still wasn't positive what Meeka's plans were. Either way, I didn't want to be caught out in the streets alone again for a round two of what happened before. Though I felt better about not having to hit the bars as much, I was bored. I didn't want to spend my time with Dyna, so I would find anything to do to avoid being around her. Soon, she was realizing that I was purposely staying away from her, and she wasted no time confronting me about it.

I had just come to the office to try and help with the on-line clients. I was exhausted; for some reason, I tossed and turned all night the night before.

"We need to talk before you start working," Dyna said as I headed toward the desk.

"Talk about what?" I asked, annoyed. Some days even the sound of her voice made my skin crawl.

"About how you keep avoiding me. What's your problem?"

"There is no problem. I'm just trying to work without aggravation."

"Aggravation? So you're saying I'm getting on your nerves or something?"

"I didn't say that, Dyna!"

"You might as well have! You know I do too much for you to have to kiss your ass. You should be thanking me every day for helping you stay away from your fucked up family!"

"Dyna, I'm not in the mood to argue with you today, or any other day for that matter. I just want to work, and if you won't allow me to do that in peace, then I'll go back home!" I was tired of arguing with her when things didn't go her way. I wanted things to go my way for a change.

"Fine, then leave!" she yelled back.

I turned around and headed toward the door. I believed in my heart that our relationship was over. There wasn't anything left to fight for. She obviously didn't care too much for me. I was just a trophy to her. The little ghetto girl that she'd made all better. Well, I wasn't better, and the only way that I would be better was to get far away from her.

After leaving the office I decided to head down to the community college to get a catalog. I really didn't have an idea of what I wanted to take in school, but I figured with some of my free time I could browse through the book and see what jumped out at me. The lobby of the college wasn't too crowded, so I was able to quickly make my way through to the display that held the catalogs. I picked up an application as well to hold onto until I was really ready to start school.

That evening, I stayed in and began flipping through the catalog. Dyna came home and noticed what I was looking at. Instead of responding, she gave me a killer look and walked past me without saying a word. I was surprised that she didn't try to discourage me or break me down, especially since she was pissed that I had been ignoring her. School would definitely take me away from her and I was sure she wouldn't like it. She would feel just as she would feel if it was a person taking me away.

Two months after the beating incident I went out clubbing on a Saturday night with Jenna. We hadn't really hung out as much since Dyna and I became a couple. I had to practically drag Jenna along because her fear of being fired almost took over her need to have fun. We agreed on a club, and after getting dressed I left the house without giving Dyna any information about where my destination was.

Once we passed the long line and made our way into

the crowded club, we headed straight to the bar for the buzz we needed to set the party off. My drink of choice was Hennessy and Coke while Jenna settled for an apple martini. I had consumed so much liquor since I'd been working for Dyna that fruity drinks did nothing for my alcohol appetite. After taking two drinks to the head, I decided to go dance. I stepped onto the dance floor and began to dance sensuously all alone until Jenna joined me. We danced while everyone around us pointed and stared. I didn't care what people thought. I was enjoying myself.

Jenna and I danced with each other three songs straight until I decided to take a bathroom break. On my way out of the bathroom someone tapped me on my shoulder.

"So, it is you that got everyone in here in an uproar? I knew it had to be you," Mya said, smiling.

"What's up? How are you?"

"I'm cool. I'm glad to see that you are OK. I heard about what happened to you. I didn't know how to get in touch with you to see how you were."

"Yeah, I'm cool now. Just trying to work to save this money for college."

"You still want to go to college?"

"Yeah, I do. So, what are you doing at the club pregnant?"

"Marlo was tripping, and I didn't have anything else to do, so I decided to hang out. I'm surprised to see you here. I didn't think you came around these parts anymore."

"I haven't forgotten about where I came from, trust me. It's not enough money in the world for that."

"So, who's the chick you were all up on out there? Your new girlfriend?"

"Naw, that's just my friend. I'm still with Dyna, even though I don't really want to be."

"Well that's kind of how my situation is. But I really want us to keep in touch so we can catch up. I miss you."

"Yeah, I miss you too. I'll call you and make sure we hang out soon. You take care of yourself and that baby. You definitely need to stay out of these clubs!"

"Ok, I will. You take care of yourself too," she said before hugging me and walking toward the exit of the club.

I made my way through the crowd and found Jenna. We danced a little more before leaving the club. I decided to crash at Jenna's place since I was too drunk to drive home. Plus I was in no condition to argue with Dyna about where I had been. Jenna lived in a two-bedroom apartment in South Philly. It was the first time I had actually been inside her apartment. I had dropped her off a few times, but I never got out of the car. I dropped down into the first chair by the door.

"That liquor really messed you up?" Jenna asked with a giggle.

"Plus the fact that I haven't been sleeping that much lately. Wondering when that crazy chick will come in and try something else," I said, failing at my attempt to take off my shoes.

"Here, let me help you," Jenna said, assisting me.

"Thanks."

"You know, it's a shame the way that Dyna reacted to that whole situation. I would have thought it would have really made her put her foot down with Meeka. I thought that she really cared about you."

"Yeah, I did too."

"Well, you can always crash here when you don't want to go home," she said, placing her hand on my thigh.

Before then I had never looked at Jenna the way that I did at that moment. Maybe it was the effects of the alcohol or the disarray my relationship with Dyna was in. It was hard to understand the feelings, but I couldn't resist them. I leaned in to kiss her, and our tongues met instantly and massaged the other. She used my thigh as a guide to find my kitty, which was throbbing with excitement. She moved my panties to the side and touched my clit with her fingers. I could have exploded instantly, but I held my composure as I enjoyed the French kiss. She moved from my clit to my tunnel and stuck her fingers inside until she found my G-spot. She continued the motion, causing me to orgasm within minutes. I was paralyzed as she removed her skirt and panties. I rubbed on my breasts as she climbed onto the chair with her wetness over my face. I stuck out my tongue and waited for her to sit. I moved my tongue back and forth as she continued in a grinding motion until she came all over my face. The taste was wonderful, and it was one that I would remember. I figured I would probably feel guilty for what just happened once I sobered up, but for now I was content. It wasn't hard for me to fall asleep because I was exhausted, and the feeling of Jenna's warm body next to mine made me feel secure. Security was something Dyna wasn't able to offer me, and I knew it wouldn't be long before our relationship ended for good. Things had gone from bad to worse, and all I could do was hope that she would let me go without any drama.

The next morning when I woke up I was a little unsure of where I was, but I soon remembered the previous night's events. I could smell the aroma of breakfast, which made my stomach growl even harder than it had as I tossed and turned in bed. I got up and found the bathroom before making my way to the kitchen. I was shocked at how bad I looked and was almost afraid to go outside. Jenna had prepared a feast for breakfast and set the table for two. She smiled when she noticed me and made her way over to hug and kiss me. I felt a little awkward as she wrapped her arms around my waist. Though I had enjoyed our sexual endeavor, I didn't want her to assume that we would be in a relationship. I wasn't even completely done with Dyna, and I had learned that it wasn't wise to jump from one bed to another.

"So, did you enjoy yourself last night?" she asked with a grin.

"Yeah, it was good."

"Shit, it was great. It's been a while since I was with a woman. My man would flip if he knew I was going down that road again."

Glad that she was still in a relationship, but curious about the comment I asked, "What do you mean down that road again?"

"Girl, me and him used to do threesomes all the time, but once I started fucking women on my own time he didn't like that shit. He can't eat my pussy the way a woman can. Shit, they know how to lick it and make you feel good. Don't get me wrong; I do love dick, but I love women too. You feel me?" she asked, grabbing a plate from the cabinet.

"Yeah, I know what you mean."

"Well, I want us to still remain friends, and I don't want you to think that I'm going to be all up on you to be with you. So don't even worry. Dyna will never find out, OK?"

"OK," I said, relieved as I began to put food on my plate.

"So are you going home when you leave here?"

"Yeah, I'm prepared for an argument, though, since I didn't come home last night."

"That's crazy, Sugar. When are you going to leave her ass alone so her and that crazy bitch can be together?"

"I know, it's just a little hard to just walk away when I work for her. I need the money, and I don't have enough saved to quit. I'm sure she'd fire me if I did that."

"Probably not. That's too easy for her. She's the type of person that will make your life miserable."

"Well, she's already succeeded at that!"

After we finished breakfast, I decided to be on my way home, and I wasn't surprised when I pulled up and found Dyna's car in the driveway. I knew that instead of going to work that she would wait until I came in just to argue. I unlocked the door to find her sitting in the living room on the sofa. I braced myself for what I knew was coming next.

"Where the fuck were you all night?" she yelled, rising from the sofa and walking in my direction.

"Out!"

"Don't be smart. I know you were out! Did you fuck somebody?"

"No, I didn't, Dyna. I stayed at Jenna's because I was too tired to drive home."

"Bullshit, Sugar! You fucked her didn't you?" she yelled.

"I already told you where I was, and I said no the first time you asked me that."

"Who the fuck are you talking to? Don't forget that I made your ass. You wouldn't have shit if it weren't for me. You'd still be living there in that dirty-ass apartment with your crackhead mother!"

"Dyna, I really don't feel like arguing with you right now."

"Well, you don't have a choice, because I'm not finished talking. I want to know what's going on with you lately."

"What's going on with me? What's going on with you? You are the one that's been acting funny. I should be asking you if you fucked somebody. Somebody like Meeka perhaps!"

"What? I think that you've forgotten who pays the bills," she said pointing her index finger in my face.

"No, I haven't. You've made sure of that," I said, sarcastically.

"If I didn't love you, I'd put your ass out on the street right now. I've put too much money out for you to let my investment go to waste."

"Investment? What the hell do you mean by that?"

"What do you think I mean? Do you think I'd kick out all of my money for nothing?" she laughed. "I guess you really are naive! But you'll see," she said before walking to the door. "I hope you're not too drunk to bring your ass to work! I'll see you in an hour and don't be late," she spoke sternly as she exited the house.

I stood there trying to figure out what she meant when she said that I would see. Obviously it was meant as a threat, but of what? I guessed Jenna was right when she said that Dyna would make me miserable. **Things had definitely gone from bad to worse.** I just had to watch her closely for her next move.

Chapter 7

New Intentions

Regaining my close relationship with Mya was some-thing that I set out to do. I knew it wasn't truly her fault that my mother abused me. I could no longer blame her for something that probably wouldn't have been different even if Mya walked the straight line. I began picking her up on days when I was free just to hang out and talk. I learned a lot about her, and I also learned why she behaved the way she did when we were growing up. She said that she was always jealous of me because I was smart and she knew I would be successful. Her over-the-top actions were to get attention, but instead I received it. Though it was negative attention my mother gave me, Mya never got any—good or bad.

Mya had recently dropped out of school, and I tried my best to encourage her to return. Unfortunately, she had already made up her mind, and since Marlo was cool with her decision to quit school to raise their child, she was happy. The only option I had was to accept it.

My relationship with Dyna was becoming even more

strained as my relationship with Mya grew close again. Throughout our relationship, Dyna had been encouraging me to patch up things with my sister, but now she appeared to be jealous. I believed that she only encouraged it because she never thought it would happen anyway. I think that's why Dyna encouraged me to do a lot of things. Dyna was definitely getting more controlling and jealous. My plan to move away from her wasn't really working since she still wasn't trying to let me go. The arguments never stopped, and now that I was hanging out with Mya, they intensified.

One particular outing with Mya led to a huge argument, and it was one that I didn't see coming. Mya asked me to accompany her to an ultrasound, and I took off for the day to go since Marlo wasn't able to go with her. I left Dyna a message with the details of my destination, and after getting dressed I went to pick Mya up. I returned home around 7:00, after Mya and I went out Chili's for dinner. Dyna was home sitting in the living room watching TV when I arrived.

"It takes that long for an ultrasound?" she asked, looking down at her watch, noting the time.

"No it doesn't," I replied, annoyed.

"Well, where were you?"

"We went out to eat after the doctor's appointment."

"Out to eat? After you skipped out on work? I hope you know your not getting paid for today."

"I didn't expect to."

"Well good, tell that bitch to pay you!"

"What the fuck is wrong with you, Dyna?" I yelled.

"I'm tired of fucking around with you, Sugar, and I've decided that your job in promotion isn't good enough. You need to start going on dates, or I'm going to reduce your pay. You need to start paying rent too, because this shit with me and you is over."

"Is that right?" I asked, surprised.

"Yeah, so effective immediately, I'll start arranging your dates."

"I thought you loved me, Dyna. You promised that I would never have to escort." I pleaded. I was happy that she wanted to end the relationship, but devastated that she wanted me to sell my body.

"Well, you promised to be loyal to me too."

"I have been."

"No, you've been far from loyal, and this conversation is over. I've already moved your stuff back into the spare room, and just so you know, Meeka's moving back in."

"What?" I asked, as I began to cry. Though I was tired of Dyna and ready to move on I wasn't ready to live on my own and I knew that I couldn't stay there with Meeka. I did care about Dyna and at this point didn't even know why. I was angry that she would force me to degrade myself. But what was I supposed to do? I had been spending my money just as quick as I got it and I didn't have enough saved to do anything else.

"Don't cry now, it's too late for tears."

I decided not to say anything else to make the situation any worse. I turned my back and made my way up to the spare room. I opened the door to find my things scattered all over the bed and floor. I cried as I began to pick up my things and fold them. Though I was glad that my relationship with Dyna was over I never expected it to end with Dyna forcing me to be a prostitute. I agreed to work for her under the condition that I would never have to prostitute myself. I knew that I didn't have enough money saved to move out, but I refused to live under the same roof as

Meeka. I called Jenna and explained the situation, and, of course, she wasn't at all surprised. I planned to stay at Jenna's until I could get enough money together to move into my own place. I slept lightly that night, afraid of what would happen next.

The following morning when I woke up there was an itinerary laid out on my nightstand. It started out with a salon appointment for hair and nails, followed by a boutique appointment for an outfit and lingerie. I had assisted Dyna with planning these itineraries for the other girls for their dates. Basically she sent you to be dressed to the customer's specifications. It's like when you order a meal at a restaurant, you tell the waiter how you want you steak—rare, medium, or well done. These customers would explain the way they wanted the girl to look, dress, and even smell, and Dyna would make sure that she fulfilled their wishes to keep them coming back. It gave me chills looking at the 5:00 meeting at the Doubletree hotel, but I sucked it up and decided that I couldn't let Dyna know she was getting the best of me.

I showered and made the drive to the salon. When I entered all eyes were on me, and I assumed they were all surprised to see me. I waved hello to everyone and held my head up high, not letting on that I was ashamed of what I was about to do. Lisa was the stylist who would be working with me, and I walked to her station in the back of the salon.

"What's up, girl? I never expected to see you in here," Lisa said as she hugged me.

"Yeah, me either. But I'm here, girl, so, hook me up!"

"I know that's right," she said, smiling.

"So what are you going to do with me today?"

"Girl, not much, you know you're the shit anyway! The customer just wants you to look natural. I'm going to do a wet and wavy look in your hair with some highlights to accentuate your skin."

"Oh, OK. Do you know if the customer is male or female?"

"I think it's male."

"OK."

It had been a so long since I was with a man I was kind of looking forward to it now. About two hours later, I left the salon with a new look, and I actually loved it. I went to the boutique next and was greeted by the owner. She pulled out a strapless black dress that hugged my curves perfectly and some black strappy sandals. I was dressed to impress and now on my way up Roosevelt Boulevard to meet the man who was definitely going to get his money's worth.

I was nervous as I approached Room 214. I stood there for a second, contemplating knocking. I knew this would open a whole new world of sin. I put my hand to the door and lightly knocked. About five seconds later I heard footsteps moving toward the door and the butterflies in my stomach were driving me crazy. As the door opened, I took a deep breath.

"Sugar!"

"Marlo! What the hell are you doing here?" I asked, embarrassed that he was the one behind the door.

"I'm ready to ask you the same question?"

"I know that you are not who I am supposed to meet here? I knew that bitch would find a way to degrade me even more."

"What are you talking about?" he asked confused.

"Dyna is forcing me to do this shit and her setting me up with you is just another way to get back at me," I said as tears began to flow.

"Come in, Sugar, so we can talk," he instructed.

"I can't believe her," I made my way to the chair to sit.

"What's going on? I didn't even know you worked for her."

"I never escorted before. I was just doing the promotion until she got tired of me and decided to make me do this. This is the first date she sent me on."

"Damn, that's messed up. So did you want to do it?"

"Hell no! I've only had sex with four people in my life, and now she wants me to have sex with different people every day. I'm going to try to make the best of it, because I'm not going to let her break me down."

"Well that's a good attitude, but that still means that you have to escort every night."

"I know. Well I'm glad that it was you today so I can skip tonight at least. I'll pay you back what she paid you if you want me to."

"No, that's cool. We can just chill here and talk."

"Come to think of it, what's up with you getting an escort? What's going on with you and Mya?"

"We're not together anymore."

"What? She didn't tell me that." Mya told me things were rocky but she didn't say that they were broken up.

"That's because she keeps trying to get back with me."

"So what happened?"

"Well you know your sister. You can't tame her, and she's all over the place."

"What do you mean all over the place?"

"I can't really get into all the details because it pisses me off when I think about it, but I tell you one thing, though I did my dirt, she did the ultimate, and it ain't no going back after that."

"So why can't you tell me what she did?"

"Because she should tell you. I'm not trying to bash her

or make her look bad at all. I'll always care about her, and I'll always be there for my child."

"She'll probably never tell me the truth, Marlo. She hasn't even told me that y'all broke up."

"Well, hopefully one day she will. So what happened with you and that nigga JT?" he asked, quickly changing the subject.

"He was a nut. He tried to set me up. You can't trust slimy dudes like him."

"I could have told you that if you would have asked me. That dude is known for that type of shit."

"Well, I wish I would have asked for your advice, because you're really cool. I never would have guessed that we could sit and chat like this."

"Me either," he laughed.

"And just think, you came here to get some head and got stuck with me and all of my drama."

"It's cool. She only charged me $100 for tonight. I thought it was kind of strange, but if you want I can keep paying her so you won't have to go out on those dates. We could just meet here and chill."

"You would do that for me? How can you afford that?" I asked

"You know I'm a boss in this city. I got money coming out of my ears!" he laughed. "That's the least I can do for you."

"Well, I appreciate it. I still can't believe that you are out here about to pay for sex. Why? You should have women falling all over you."

"I'm busy watching my blocks. I don't have time to be chasing no females. Then you gotta wine them and dine them just to get some. Shit, I can just call Dyna up and have a chick meet me here. No strings attached. It's just easier that way."

"But what about Mya? You really don't plan to get back with her?"

"No, I don't. She's not the one for me. I've learned that, and it was definitely the hard way. Love is a bitch, you know. It will knock you right on the ass if you let it."

"I definitely know what you mean. I'm going to have to pay you back for this, Marlo. I don't even feel comfortable taking your money like that."

"I told you it's no big deal, but if it will make you feel better, you can pay me back whenever you can afford to. Deal?" He put out his hand for me to shake it.

"Deal," I agreed.

We sat and talked all night, and I learned a lot about Marlo. I was surprised that Mya could let a man like him slip away. I couldn't imagine what she did that was as bad as he described. I wished it had been me that Marlo wanted that day at the bus stop. My life would be a lot different right now. It meant a lot to me that Marlo would protect me by paying for me each night until I was able to walk away from Dyna completely. I left the hotel that night with a smile, and I also looked forward to coming back each night to learn more about Marlo.

Once I reached Dyna's house I noticed Meeka's car in the driveway. I entered the house with caution and noticed the two of them in the kitchen. I decided to go say hello with a big-ass smile on my face to let her know that she didn't get the effect that she wanted.

"Good evening, ladies," I said as I opened the refrigerator and removed a spring water.

"What the hell are you so happy about?" Dyna asked.

"I'm alive, that's all! Good-night," I said as I left the kitchen and headed upstairs to bed.

I fell asleep shortly after I showered and when I woke up the next morning my itinerary was basically the same as the day before and it would remain that way for the next three weeks. I still hadn't found out from Mya what happened with Marlo, and I had been just as unsuccessful finding out from him. She continued to tell me lies about her relationship, and I continued to leave out the fact that I had been spending time with him every night for over three weeks.

Though it began innocent, I was beginning to have feelings for him that I knew were wrong. We would lie next to each other in bed every night and I would fall asleep smelling his Issey Miyake cologne. I would lay my head on his muscular chest and dream of a better life. I dreamed of him making love to me and telling me that I belonged to him. Each day I went there with a smile—even with the unsettling thought of betraying Mya in mind. We hadn't had sex, and we hadn't even kissed, but I dreamed about it. I knew if Mya found out she would be just as upset about the thought as with the action. Again, I was yearning for attention, and in the past that was definitely something that got me in trouble. I didn't know how long I could control myself around him, so I knew sooner or later I would have to find another way to get paid. That way I could pay him back and quit working at Dyna's.

I went to the hotel room that we always stayed in and he was there waiting for me with dinner on the table. I smiled when I noticed the candlelight and champagne.

"What's all of this for? Are we celebrating something?" I asked.

"As a matter of fact, we are," he said, helping me remove my coat.

"So what's going on?" I asked as he guided me to the table.

"Look, we've been coming here for three weeks now, and I know how much you want to leave your job and get your own spot. I just bought a duplex out Yeadon, and I'm going to let you stay in one of the apartments for free until you get on your feet."

"Wow, are you serious?" I hugged him.

"Very serious," he said, looking into my eyes with his arms still wrapped around the small of my back. "You know the day that I met Mya at that bus stop?"

"Yeah, I remember."

"When I called out, I was actually calling for you. I noticed your innocence and your natural beauty. That was something that I'd never had in my life. I only talked to Mya because she came over to the car first, and once I saw the look on your face I knew that I would probably never get the chance to get with you after that. When I found out that you were her sister I was glad because I knew that we could be cool one day. I need special people like you in my life."

"Are you serious, Marlo? You really wanted me?" I asked, stunned.

"Yeah, I am. I was feeling you since day one."

At that moment I couldn't resist the temptation any more. I had always been attracted to Marlo, and now to hear that he felt the same, there was no way I could continue just being his friend. I moved closer to him. As our lips touched, we both stared, contemplating the next move. I stuck my tongue out just enough to taste his lips. He tightened his grip around my waist so I could feel his hardness through his jeans. I moaned as he began to massage my tongue with his. I could feel my panties getting wet as I unhooked his belt and unzipped his pants to free his manhood. I pulled his swollen member through his boxers and stroked it with my hand. He pulled my shirt up over my breasts and sucked on my protruding nipples. I moved down on my knees and licked his length before taking him into my mouth. I became more excited as his moans of delight became louder. I worked my hands and mouth so good he pulled away.

"Damn, you're trying to make me cum early, huh?"

I smiled.

He guided me to the bed, where he didn't waste any time feasting on my already wet fruit. I screamed with joy as I had two consecutive orgasms. Marlo was working wonders with his tongue, and my body was yearning for him to dive deep inside of me.

"You like that shit?" he asked as his fingers were moving around inside of me, touching my G-spot.

"Yes," I moaned before biting my bottom lip. "I need to feel you inside of me!"

He continued to lick my pearl. "You need me, baby?"

"Yes, I need you."

Marlo soon rose up and began to rub my clit with the head of his pole. I wanted to feel his length, and I moved my hips to make way for his entry. I was excited as he gently plunged deep inside of me, instantly causing another orgasm. His movements were hitting all of the right places and I was definitely going to need more of him.

"That's my spot right there," I said as he sucked on my neck, causing me to exude more lubrication. He continued moving in and out of me as I used my nails to dig into his back. As his speed increased, I knew he was about to explode soon. I held on to him tightly as he released every drop. We were both exhausted and unsure of what to say next. As he lay beside me, I stared at the ceiling and wondered how this would change my future. I wasn't sure what to expect because I wasn't sure what he was thinking. I knew that what we did was wrong but it felt so good. It felt like things were supposed to happen this way. Then I thought about Mya and her baby.

Damn, I let my temptation take over. I betrayed my sister in the worst way.

"Are you OK?" he asked, sitting up on the edge of the bed.

"Yeah, I'm good. How about you?"

"I'm cool."

"So where do we go from here?"

"Wherever you want. I'm down for whatever," he said, smiling.

"I have strong feelings for you, Marlo, but I don't want to be selfish and ruin your life."

"How could you possibly ruin my life?"

"You and Mya, I don't want to step on her toes, and now that we've gotten sort of close again, I know that this would ruin everything."

"Well it's up to you. I told you that me and her are through. I'm not really concerned about her finding out, but if you are, I understand. I'm happy about what just happened. I mean, that shit was great, but I don't want to be pushy. I want you to want me before things go any further."

"I do want you, Marlo. I'm just afraid of getting hurt."

Placing his hand on top of mine and glancing into my eyes, he said, "I would never hurt you. I wish I could have caught you a long time ago—before anyone got a chance to hurt you, and then you wouldn't have a reason to be afraid. I want to love you. I have never been as happy as I've been just being around you the last few weeks. I know you're honest, and I know your love would be sincere. I'm trying to experience all of that."

"You know I've been through a lot, Marlo. Growing up was rough, and life after that hasn't been much of a party."

"Well, let me ask you something, and if you don't want to answer me, I truly understand."

"OK, what is it?"

"I know that you were abused by your mom growing up, but what about your dad? Did he ever do anything to hurt you?"

"No, the only thing that he did to hurt me was to ignore my mother's actions. I hate that he didn't step in and protect me."

"So, do you think that has anything to do with the way you look at relationships?"

"No, I've forgiven my dad because I know he was never in his right mind either. Both of them were on drugs heavy. I know that had he been clean from drugs he would have stepped in."

"Well, it takes a strong person to forgive things like that, because I know if those things would have happened to me, I probably wouldn't be able to forgive my parents. I'm just glad you haven't let that affect the way you view men or relationships in general."

"No, I haven't let any of that affect the way that I view anything, and not just relationships."

"So, what do you want to do? Because if you really want to be with me, you can leave that Dyna bitch alone and I will make sure that you're OK money-wise, I promise you that. You don't even have to get any of your shit from her house. I'll buy you all new shit."

"I do want to be with you, I really do. Do you really think that things can work with us?"

"I know they'll work. Anything I put my mind to always works," he said, moving close to me and gently kissing me on my forehead.

My body was yearning for more, and I slowly began to

massage his hardened pole. It wasn't long before he was deep inside of me and we were wrapped around each other. That night I slept with a sense of peace. I knew that when I woke up a new life would begin. I had never expected to end up with Marlo, and though I was happy about it, I had to figure out how I could hide it from Mya. I knew I couldn't hide our relationship forever, but I had to make sure that when she did find out, it wouldn't blow up in my face. I was excited about calling Dyna and letting her know that I would no longer be her employee. I could have the weight of Dyna's control lifted off of my shoulder. After leaving my mom, I never thought anyone would be able to control me the way she had. I let Dyna in and she took advantage of my weaknesses. I could now move on and hopefully never have to see her again.

After leaving the hotel, I decided to drive to Dyna's office. I decided that a face-to-face meeting would be much more effective than a phone conversation. I was smiling from ear to ear as I made my way through the store and up the stairs that led to the office. I wasn't really nervous, but I had butterflies in my stomach. I knocked on the door before going in, and once I opened the door and noticed Dyna's surprised expression, it was much easier to relay the information. I walked over to one of the chairs directly in front of her desk.

"So what brings you here?" she asked as she continued to type up itineraries for the day.

"I'm here to let you know that I will no longer be working for you."

"What?" She now turned her attention to me. "What the fuck do you mean you won't be working for me anymore?"

"It's just like that; I'm not going to degrade myself anymore. I'm done!" I said as I stood up from the chair.

Shaking her head in disbelief, Dyna stood up from her chair and pointed her fingers in my direction. "I made you. You owe me! If I never picked your broke ass up, you wouldn't have shit right now. I don't know how you think you are going to survive. Did Marlo promise you the world? Don't forget, that's your sister's man!"

"This has nothing to do with Marlo, and the way you tried to degrade me even more by setting me up on a date with him only made me stronger."

"Whatever, Sugar. You'll need me, and don't even think about coming to get your things from my house now, because they won't be there!" she said before sitting down in her chair and frowning. "I should have listened to Meeka from day one when she told me not to trust you. I should have known that you would betray me."

"Dyna I didn't betray you. You changed, and so did I. I'm moving on now, and that's what's best for me."

"You don't know what's best for you. You've been fucking your sister's man for weeks, and you think that's the way to a new life. Give me a break," she said flagging her hand at me. "If you know what is best for you, you will have your ass at work tonight!"

"I've already told you that I quit. I was trying to end this on a nice note, but I see you are only going to make things difficult. And just to let you know, I don't need anything from your house. I'll be fine," I said, making my way to the door. "And another thing, he's not her man. He's mine!"

I walked out the door and closed the chapter of my life that had caused me so much pain. I could hear her throwing things at the door as I walked down the steps.

I was done with Dyna, and to prove that to her, I didn't even take the car that she had bought me. I left it parked in front of her store for her to see when she walked out of the building. I called Marlo as I walked to the nearest bus stop to head to Jenna's apartment to hang out until Marlo could show me the new apartment.

"Hey Sugar, what's up?" he said, as he answered the phone.

"Nothing much, I'm on my way to the bus stop to go home."

"Bus stop? Where is your car?" he asked.

"I left it at Dyna's store. I had to let her know that I didn't need her anymore."

"You shouldn't have done that," he said, in a low tone.

"Why not? We are going to be together right?" I asked, with concern.

"About that. I really like you a lot, Sugar, but I'm just not sure how things could work."

"What are you talking about? Just last night you said that you wanted to be with me, what happened?" I said, as a tear fell from my eye.

"Sugar, I'm sorry. I have to go handle some business right now, but I'll call you later so we can finish talking."

"Don't even bother, Marlo. You're just like everyone else!" I said before hanging up.

I felt like the biggest fool in the world. I had believed in Marlo, and just that quick he disappointed me. I wasn't sure what to do next since I had walked out on the only employment I had. When I made it to Jenna's apartment I was depressed, and it showed. I was upset that I had again made a decision that could make my future a little harder to get through. I had been hurt once again, and I needed to really think about my next step. **My new intentions** were to better myself without the help of anyone else. I needed to take care of me for once!

Chapter 8

One More Chance

For the next couple of weeks I went out job hunting almost every day. I mostly went to the malls because my only job experience before Dyna's was in retail. I didn't think it would be hard to find another job. Since I had gotten used to making thousands of dollars each week, I couldn't find a job that suited my interest. I had a little money saved, but I didn't want to touch it because I was still going to go to college once I got things in order. I was slowly moving on, and I felt freedom for the first time in my life. Jenna continued to work at Dymes while I continued to struggle with finding a job that I enjoyed. Jenna was nice enough to let me stay with her until I was able to get on my feet. After hitting all of the malls, I would go home and search the newspaper classifieds. It was becoming such a routine that it seemed like a job to find a job. I hadn't talked to Mya much since she gave birth to a baby boy a week earlier. I went to see her at the hospital and was turned off seeing Marlo by her side like they were one

big, happy family. I could tell that it made him just as uncomfortable as it made me. Mya had called me while I was
out at the mall to let me know of the new arrival.

"Hello," I said as I headed out of the Old Navy store.

"Hey, sis. Just called to tell you that you have a new
nephew!"

"Really? Congratulations! I'm out at the mall now, but I
will stop by when I'm done here. What hospital are you
in?"

"University of Penn," she replied.

"OK, I'll see you soon"

After I hung up with her I stopped by the Hallmark
store to pick her up a little gift. Then I caught the bus
down to the hospital. I entered the room with a teddy bear
and flowers, and as soon as Marlo and I made eye contact,
we quickly looked away from each other.

"Hey, big sis. I'm glad you could come."

"You know I wouldn't miss this for the world," I said,
hugging her.

"I'm going to go out to the car and let y'all talk, baby.
I'll be back in a few," Marlo said before kissing her and
walking out of the room.

I cringed at the sight of him kissing her. "So, how was
the delivery?"

"Crazy! Not as bad as before, but it was still rough."

"I can't believe my little sister has another baby."

"Yeah, me either, but you have to go by the nursery and
see him."

"I will now, because I have some running around to do.
I just wanted to stop by and show my face."

"Well, thanks for coming. Call me tomorrow, OK?"

"I will," I said, hugging her once more.

I waved goodbye as I left the room. On my way to the
bus stop I noticed Marlo standing on the corner smoking

a cigarette. As I walked up he tried to act as if he didn't see me coming.

"Playing father of the year now, I see."

"I guess so," he said, avoiding eye contact.

"Why can't you look at me, Marlo?"

"Who said I couldn't look at you?"

"I'm not going to stalk you or anything, OK? Yes, I'm upset about what happened with us, but I don't hate you. I wanted to say congratulations."

"Well, thanks."

"I'll be seeing you around," I said, walking away to catch the bus.

I put on that act to show him that he didn't break me. I was hurting inside, though, because I fell for the game that he played. I cried that night because I felt that he had lied to me about his relationship with Mya. Hugging, laughing, and smiling didn't appear to be a broken relationship, and it made me sick to my stomach. I decided to steer clear of them to spare myself a little heartache.

I decided to visit Bloomingdale's since I really enjoyed working there before I met Dyna. I went back and talked to my former manager and she quickly offered me my job back. I was excited about the job, and this boosted my morale, since I had been down for so long. I went to work on my first day, which was a Monday. The day started off slow but got busy after lunch. I was setting up a new display in women's shoes when I heard a familiar voice call my name.

"So you really came back?" Marlo asked with a smile.

"Well, I didn't really have much of a choice, did I! And how did you know I was here?" I asked with sarcasm, continuing to work on my Kenneth Cole display.

"Mya told me. I miss you, Sugar," he said in that sexy tone that made me weak at the knees.

"Really? I find that hard to believe. I also find it hard to believe that you even had time to miss me since you've been playing family man."

"It wasn't even like that, Sugar. I had to be there for my son."

"You could have still been there for your son and not be with her. You lied to me, and I made a decision that could have messed up my future because of it!"

"That's not true. That decision was a good one. I know you didn't want to keep escorting, and my suggestion helped you get away from that."

"By lying to me!"

"I didn't lie to you. I meant everything that I said. My feelings for you are real."

"Whatever Marlo, I have to get back to work!"

"Look, is it OK if I take you out later so we can talk to clear some things up?"

"I don't think so!"

"Please, Sugar, let me make it up to you. I'm not with Mya. I told you I had to be there for the baby, and that's it," he begged.

"Make it up to me? I don't know if that's even possible at this point. All I see is a liar, and again, you didn't have to be with her to be there for the baby. Now, I really have to get back to work."

"Please. I promise I'll make it all good," he said as he moved close to me, letting the aroma of his cologne tickle my nose.

"Marlo, I can't take any more pain."

"It will be great. I'll pick you up at eight, OK?"

"OK, I'll give you a chance to explain. That's it, and the minute it appears to be a lie, the conversation will be over."

"I'll see you at eight then," he said before kissing me on the forehead and exiting the store.

I watched him leave and prayed that he was being honest with me. I didn't think I could stand any more disappointment. I wanted to be in love for once and with someone who was genuinely in love with me. So, I decided to give him **one more chance**.

I was excited when I left work that day, and I rushed home to figure out what I was going to wear on my date with Marlo. I tried on about ten different ensembles before deciding on one—a black dress with a low plunge in the front that showed my cleavage. I put on lotion that glittered and shoes that extended the length of my legs. I fixed my hair and make-up, put on my accessories, and waited for him to arrive. At about five after eight I heard him beep the horn. I put on a slow, sexy walk as I made my way to his new 760 BMW. I entered the car and found a comfortable place in the seat.

"You look good," he said as he licked his lips.

"Thanks," I said. "So, where are we going?"

"Somewhere special. It's a surprise."

"Oh, really?"

"Yeah, so just sit back and relax."

I did as he instructed, and we drove for what seemed like an hour. We pulled up to a large home in Phoenixville, Pennsylvania. There was a two-car garage in front and beautiful landscaping that filled the entire front lawn. I was puzzled because when he told me that he was taking me out, I thought we would go to a restaurant or something similar.

"So whose house is this?" I asked.

"Ours."

"Ours? What do you mean *ours* as if there is an *us*?"

"I brought you here to our new house. I told you I was seriously going to make everything better. Now I've taken steps to do just that; it's time to show and prove."

"Are you serious, Marlo?" I said in shock.

"Come on, let's go in," he said as he motioned with his hand.

As we entered the house, I couldn't believe how perfect everything was. I stood there for a minute, just taking in the surroundings. Marlo noticed the look on my face and began laughing hysterically.

"Are you OK?"

"I can't believe all of this, Marlo, Did you just buy this house?"

"Yeah, I did; just for you and me," he said, passing me a set of keys.

"I love it!" I said, hugging him and kissing him, sensuously hinting that I wanted to make love to him right at that moment.

"Wait, baby, we have plenty of time for that. I have one more surprise for you."

"What else could you possibly have for me?"

"Check your keys," he said, smiling and pointing to the key ring that he had given me.

I looked down, noticing a car key I looked back up at him shocked, "You didn't?" I said, looking back down at the keys.

"I did; it's in the garage."

I ran back outside and waited for him to push the button to open the garage. I began to jump up and down when I saw a brand new red BMW exactly the same as his. I turned back to him and smiled. I couldn't believe that he would do all of that for me. A few weeks ago I thought he was gone forever, and now he was all mine. I pulled

Marlo into the garage and kissed him. I pulled the garage opener from his hand and pushed the button.

As the door closed, I backed away from him and began taking off my dress. He stared at me and licked his lips as his hardened pole began to show through his jeans. I sat on the hood of the car and motioned for him to come closer to me. I placed two fingers in my mouth and then placed them inside of my wet mound as he unzipped his pants and let them drop to the ground. He lifted my legs up and pulled me closer so that my butt was right on the edge of the hood. He quickly rammed his stick inside of me, and I moaned in delight.

"You feel so good," I moaned as I sucked on his left ear.

He continued to move in and out as I continued to moan loudly. I knew from that moment that I was going to love him, and from the way that he moved, I believed that he would love me too.

After we both reached our sexual peaks, we went up to the master bedroom and showered together, and shortly after that we both fell asleep. I woke up the next morning to a ringing phone. I decided not to answer it because I wasn't ready for Mya to know about our relationship. Instead I went downstairs to hear the message that the person had left on the answering machine. I pressed the red flashing button and sat down on the arm of the sofa. There was a beep first, then the woman spoke.

"Hey, baby, it's me Julissa. I waited on you last night. I thought that you were coming over. I had it wet and hot just the way you like it too. Anyway, hit me up when you get this. Love ya!" Click.

I sat there stunned, but I didn't flip out. I Instead, I erased the message. I listened to the rest of the messages on the machine and there were more messages from her,

Mya, and a few other females. I couldn't really be pissed about people that were there before me, but I would let him know that I knew about them. I went upstairs and noticed that he had gotten up and was in the bathroom. I sat on the edge of the bed and waited for him to come out.

"Good morning," I said, smiling.

"Good morning. Who was that on the phone?" he asked.

"Julissa. I guess I ruined your plans with her last night, huh?"

"No, that girl is crazy. I never told her that I was coming over."

"Well, I'm not mad, but if you could change the number so all of your old flings can stop calling, I would appreciate it."

"I can do that," he said before kissing me. "So what were your plans for today?" he asked, sitting down on the bed next to me.

"I didn't have any plans. I'm off work today. Why?"

"Take this, and go get you some new stuff," he said, passing me two MasterCard gift cards.

"How much is here to spend?" I asked.

"It's five gees. $2,500 apiece. So have fun on me!"

"Thank you so much!" I said, hugging him. "So, what are you doing today?"

"The usual work—watching my blocks. But I'm going to go get my little shorty this morning first and hang out with him for a couple hours."

"Oh, OK. Well, I'm going to get dressed now so I can go spend this money," I said, laughing.

It didn't take me long to get dressed and rush out of the house. Marlo had left a little while before I did. I was on my way to Jenna's to show her my new car when my cell phone rang. I glanced at the caller ID and recognized the number as Mya's.

"Hello," I said, uneasy.

"Hey, what's up?"

"Nothing, on my way to the mall!"

"For real? I was looking for something to do since Marlo just came and got the baby. I'm broke, but come pick me up and I'll go with you."

"OK."

I hung up and made the detour to pick her up. I was nervous about the meeting, and I hoped she wouldn't be able to tell from my actions. I pulled up in front of the building and beeped the horn. Noticing the look on her face when she came outside and saw the new car, I quickly began to think of what story I was going to tell. Mya was aware of the fact that I had quit working for Dyna, and she also knew I had been working at Bloomingdale's since then. Bloomingdale's was definitely not enough money to buy a BMW. She stood outside the car staring as I rolled down the window.

"When did you get this?" she asked, pointing at the car in shock.

"Yesterday."

"How the hell can you afford this?"

"I had a little money saved for a down payment. My credit is pretty cool, so the car payment isn't that high. Come on, get in," I said, motioning with my hand for her to get in.

"Girl, Marlo has a car just like this, but his is black."

"For real?" I said, playing dumb.

"Yeah, but that's what's up. You deserve it. So what mall are we going to?"

"King of Prussia. Is that cool?"

"I ain't buying anything anyway, so any mall is cool."

I decided to question her about Marlo again to see if anything had changed since the last time I asked. I hoped that I would find out what happened when they broke up the first time since I had been unsuccessful thus far.

"So, what's up with you and Marlo anyway?"

"Not a damn thing! I think he has a new girlfriend now. I doubt if we'll ever get back together."

"Well, what happened?"

"I don't like to talk about it. It's a messed up situation that could ruin a lot of lives."

"Damn, well what's that bad that you can't tell me?"

"One day I'll tell you, but right now I'm not ready."

"I understand, but do you want him back?"

"I love him with all of my heart, but I know I hurt him and things would never be the same, so I've come to terms with that."

"I didn't know it was that bad."

"It's OK. It was my fault, so I had to let him go. Hopefully the one he's with will do a better job at making him happy then I did. "

I knew then that I would probably never find out what happened between the two of them, so I decided to let it go. After we reached the mall, I went crazy spending the money that Marlo had given me along with a little of my own. Mya noticed the gift cards and commented that Marlo used to give her gift cards all the time to go shopping. I think that she got suspicious, but I tried to brush it off, hoping that the list of clues wouldn't put up a red flag about Marlo and me. I tried to move off the subject by suggesting that we go to the food court to eat, and she agreed. After ordering our food and finding a table to sit down at, we continued our small talk until we were interrupted by my ringing cell phone.

"Hello," I said without checking the caller ID.

"Hey, baby. What's up?" Marlo spoke gently.

"Having fun spending your money, I can really get used to this," I said, laughing.

"You will get used to it, because that's one of the things that I like doing for my woman."

"Good. Well, I'm out at the mall with my sister, so I'll call you when I'm done, OK? Don't miss me too much!"

"Damn, she's with you?" he asked.

"Yeah."

"All right, just call me when you're done."

"Cool!" I said before hanging up.

"A new man?" Mya asked.

"Yeah, well I just got with him."

"Oh, OK. That's nice," she replied blandly.

I assumed that his phone call would have been another hint to her, but it didn't appear to be. The rest of the shopping trip went off without a hitch, and I dropped Mya back off at home before I went back to my new house to put away my things. While hanging all of my new clothing up in the closet, my cell phone rang again and it was Dyna. I was a little hesitant about answering it, but I knew that she would probably just keep calling back if I didn't.

"Hello!" I yelled into the phone after I pressed talk.

"What's up, stranger? How are things going?" she said sarcastically.

"Great, as a matter of fact!" I responded.

"Well, I wonder how great things will be when Mya finds out that you are fucking her baby's father?"

"What?"

"Yeah, you know you owe me some work, and unless you come back to work for me, I'll make sure she finds out."

"Is that supposed to scare me?"

"Don't think I won't do it," she warned.

"Do whatever you want to, Dyna. I'm not coming to work for you, and if you tell her I'll just deal with it. Have a nice life!" I said, before ending the call.

"Fuck!" I yelled as I sat down on the bed. I knew Dyna would keep trying to ruin my life. I knew she was serious about telling Mya, and though I wasn't ready for her to find out, it would be a relief. It would mean that everyone could know about our relationship, and we wouldn't have to hide it. I called Marlo and told him what Dyna said, and he wasn't worried. He wanted Mya to know about it from day one. I, on the other hand, wasn't sure how she would react, and I didn't want to go to war with my flesh and blood. My mother was enough!

Chapter 9

Ruins . . .

The next couple of months were great. Marlo and I were happy, and Mya hadn't found out about the relationship as of yet. I was beginning to get bored with being a hustler's girl. I wanted to have my own business, and I laid out my plan to Marlo, who happily agreed to giving me the money. My business would be a gentleman's club, and I would have one of the best interior decorators to design the look. I began looking for buildings in my spare time and was unable to find one that suited my taste. I was looking for an upscale area; I didn't want it to be the average club that all of the regular around the way dudes hung out at. I also didn't want to jump on the first thing I saw, so I took my time and continued to search.

I was out looking at one property when I received a frantic call from Mya. At first I couldn't understand exactly what she was saying, but soon I heard it loud and clear. My parents had both been killed in a fire at their apartment complex and Mya needed me to meet her at the hospital. She said that my father was pronounced dead at the scene, but my mother died shortly after arriving at the hospital. I would never wish dying on anyone, and though my mother was never really good to me, I cried and was saddened by her death. I called Marlo and told him the unsettling news, and he told me that he would meet me at the hospital as well. I didn't know what to say to Mya as I arrived and noticed her sitting in tears. I sat down next to her and put my arms around her shoulder. She quickly pushed me away.

"It's all your fault," she yelled.

"What's all my fault?"

"He did it because he thought you knew!"

"Who thought I knew what?"

"He set the apartment on fire because he thought you knew about us," she cried.

"Mya, I don't know what you are talking about. What do you mean he did it because of me? "

"I know about you and Marlo, and I can't believe that you would do that to me."

"Who told you about that?"

"I saw all of the clues, the car, the gift cards, the phone calls! I'm not stupid. I told Daddy about it because I was upset, and he thought that Marlo had told you about us."

"About you and Dad? Mya, I don't understand," I asked, confused.

"I loved him so much and he killed his self because of you. I never want to see you again, Sugar! You are nothing but a lying backstabber. I hope you rot in hell!" she screamed as she rose from the bench.

"Mya, I'm sorry about Marlo, but I don't know what you mean about Dad. How could I have made him kill himself?"

"Fuck your apologies, Sugar. It won't bring them back! Why don't you ask Marlo about it? Just stay away from me,

Sugar. I never want to see your face again!" she yelled as
she walked away.

I got up from the bench still confused. I began to leave
the hospital and noticed Marlo walking in. As he got
closer to me, he put his arms out to hug me.

"I'm sorry, baby."

"She knows," I said as I hugged him back.

"She knows what?"

"About us. She said she knows. She blames me for their
deaths."

"How can she blame you for that, and what does that
have to do with you and me?"

"She kept saying something about her and my father.
Do you know what she could have been talking about?"

"I do, Sugar, but . . ."

"Marlo, I wish someone would just be honest with me,"
I said as the tears flowed from my eyes. Though I hadn't
been that close to my family, they were still my family, and
I had lost them all in one day.

"Look, let's go out to the car, and I'll tell you everything."

"OK," I agreed.

After entering his car, I took a deep breath. I was still
trying to take in the fact that both of my parents were
dead. Marlo looked at me with an unsure look on his face.
I was afraid of what he was about to say, and at that moment I wasn't sure if I really wanted to know.

"First I'm going to tell you what brought Mya and me to
an end. When Jessica was born with all of the defects I
thought damn, how am I going to deal with a sickly child?
There were so many things wrong with her that the doctors were skeptical from day one if she would live past
three months. They tried to correct as many things as they
could before doing surgery, but once everything didn't

work, surgery was the next best thing. Before the surgery they tested Mya and I both for blood type so we could donate blood just in case she needed it during surgery. After we were tested, the doctor told us that I wasn't a match, and that because of my blood type, there was no way that I could be Jessica's father. I flipped, and I wanted some answers. I could have never imagined what she told me next," he said, taking a pause.

"What?"

"Mya and your father had been having sex since she was twelve, and he was the father of her baby!"

"What? That can't be true!"

"That's what I thought, but it was, and that's the reason the baby was born with so many defects. I forgave Mya and moved on, and she promised me that she would never have sex with him again and I believed her. That's when she got pregnant again. Everything was cool until I found them a little too close one day and I had to leave her alone. That's why I asked you if your father had ever hurt you before."

"I can't believe that, Marlo. I just can't. I guess that's what she thought I knew about, and I guess that's why she blames me for his death. Damn, I should have known something was going on between the two of them. They were just too close," I said as tears began to flow. "I wish I could have helped her."

"I tried to help her. She even agreed to go to counseling, but she wanted it, Sugar, so she didn't want to be helped. It's not your fault, though. Don't ever think that."

"I know. I'm just upset that I didn't find out sooner. Now there's nothing I can do to help her since she never wants to see me again."

"She will; she'll just need some time to get over it. That's all."

"I hope you're right."

Marlo drove me to my car so I could make the drive home. Mya's heartbroken face was all I could see on the ride. I never wanted to hurt Mya, and I wished that there had been some way to soften the blow. I knew that with the death of our parents she needed a friend, and I couldn't be there for her. I wanted to go and let her lean on my shoulder and tell her that everything would be OK, and it hurt every time I thought about it. I didn't want to be blamed for their deaths because there was nothing I could have done to prevent it. I couldn't understand how she could want to continue a sexual relationship with our own father. I would have never guessed that something like that was going on. I could now understand why it was too much for Marlo to deal with. It was too much for me to deal with, and I wasn't as closely tied to the situation as him.

Once I reached the house I took a shower and lay down, and once Marlo came home he crawled in bed behind me and wrapped his arms around my waist. I loved the feeling that I got from our closeness. I had never felt that close in any other relationship I had been in. I looked forward to waking up and seeing Marlo's face. I looked forward to spending my days with him and making love to him at night. As I tried to drift off to sleep, thoughts of my mother and father flooded my mind. I wished that I had gotten a chance to say good-bye. I hadn't even seen my father since the day I left home. I was filled with so many different emotions, and after about an hour of tossing and turning, I was finally out for the count. The following day I tried to contact Mya, but was unsuccessful. I knew that she didn't have any money for a funeral, so I wanted to help out as much as I could. I used Marlo's cell phone to call her since I figured she would answer a call from him, and of course I was right.

"Hey, what's up?" she said, in a low tone.

"Mya it's Sugar. I've been trying to get in touch with you all day."

"Yeah, I know!"

"I want to give you the money for a funeral."

"Why? You didn't give a fuck about them when they were alive, so why do you care now? I'll take care of it myself."

"That's not true, Mya. I did care about them, and I want to help."

"Fuck your money, Sugar. I don't need your kind of help!"

"We are still sisters, and we are supposed to stick together."

"Bullshit! You stole the two men that I loved the most."

"I didn't steal him. You two weren't together! And I had nothing to do with what Daddy did. You're sick, Mya, You actually enjoyed sleeping with Dad? I know that I was wrong for what I did with Marlo, but you and Dad? I didn't make him set the apartment on fire."

"It's funny that you can believe that. Marlo was mine, we were working things out!"

"That's not what he told me, and that's not what you told me either!"

"He's a man, of course he'll tell you anything to get some pussy!"

"It's more than that. I'm sorry that I hurt you, but he loves me. Look what you did to him. You hurt him."

"Yeah, you're sorry all right. You're not sorry enough to let him go!" she yelled.

"Even if I did let him go, he wouldn't be with you. That wouldn't make things better for anybody."

"I really don't have anything more to say to you, so please don't call me again!"

"Mya, please!"

Click. I stared at the phone for a few seconds before giving it back to Marlo.

"What happened?" he asked.

"She still doesn't want to talk. She blames me for everything."

"I'm sorry, babe," he said, hugging me.

"I just want to help with the funeral, that's all. They were my parents too."

"Well don't worry. I'll give her the money for the funeral, OK?"

"You will?"

"Yeah, I'll give it to her. Everything will be cool. She'll forgive you."

"Thank you so much. I really appreciate it."

"I'm your man. I'm supposed to look out for you."

I felt better knowing that Mya would have the money to give them the proper burial. Even if she didn't want my help directly, she would receive it indirectly. After Marlo gave her the money he accompanied her to the funeral home to make the arrangements. At first I was a little nervous about him spending time with her, but she was the mother of his child. The funeral was set for Saturday, and I decided that I was going to go whether she wanted me to or not.

After I was dressed it took everything minus the Jaws of Life to get me out of the house. It was finally hitting me that they were really gone. Marlo practically dragged me out to the car and put me in the seat. On the long drive to the church I cried tears for all the pain that came from my parents, in life and in death. Once we entered the almost empty church I took a deep breath. We didn't have much family, but my grandmother and a few of our aunts from New York were seated in the pews. Some of their drug addict friends were seated as well. I made my way up to the closed caskets with Marlo by my side. Once I reached them, I put my hands on both of the caskets and closed my eyes. I immediately thought of the happy times, before the abuse. The times that we would all go out to the park as a family and play basketball and anything else we could think of.

Tears began to form as I heard Mya behind me whispering, "I don't why she's here. I've never known a more fake person in my life!"

I ignored her comments as I kissed my fingers and placed a kiss on each of there caskets and said, "I love you both."

As I turned to walk to be seated, I received only angry looks from the people in attendance, including my grandmother. I assumed that Mya had informed them about Marlo and me.

The funeral seemed to go on forever, and after going to the burial, we all returned to the church for the repast. Marlo and I sat at a table in the back.

I noticed Mya coming over to the table and prepared for the worst. Marlo told me that if I was ready to leave we could go. I opted to stay and hear what she had to say.

"You're not welcome here!"

"Mya, now is not the time for this."

"You just had to rub the shit in my face, didn't you? You had to come here together."

"Chill out, Mya," Marlo yelled.

"You need to leave, Sugar."

"I'll leave when I ready!" I said, standing up.

"I can assist you if you want me to."

"I wish you would touch me, Mya. That will be the last thing you touch!"

"Bitch, I will kill you!" she said, walking around the table in my direction.

"Hey, hey, hey cut this out! Your mother wouldn't want you two fighting," my grandmother instructed.

"Grandmom, I wasn't bothering her."

"What's going on with you two?" she asked us both.

"She's fucking my son's father!"

"Watch your language, young lady! Is that true, Sugar?"

"Yeah, it's true, tell her!" Mya yelled.

"She was asking me!" I retorted.

"Well, answer her, you trifling ho!"

"You know what, Mya? Fuck you! I apologized for what I did, but that's not really what this is about. You only want Marlo because Daddy's gone!" I yelled.

"Sugar, don't do this here," Marlo said, grabbing my arm.

"No, fuck that. She wants to embarrass me. Tell them, Mya, you only want Marlo back 'cause Daddy's not here to fuck you anymore!"

"What are you talking about, Sugar?" my grandmother asked, confused.

"Ask her, you see she doesn't have much to say now. She lost Marlo because she was too busy fucking our father! She even had a baby by him, now how dysfunctional is that?" I yelled as I looked around the room. Everyone was staring, and the room was so quiet that you could almost hear a pin drop.

"Mya is that true?" she asked.

Mya just stared at me with hate in her eyes before turning and running out of the church. Everyone turned and looked at me, including Marlo, who was shaking his head in disbelief.

"Why is everyone staring at me? I came here to pay my respects and she couldn't even allow me to do that. Blame it on her, not me. Marlo, let's go," I said before grabbing him by the hand and walking toward the door. I turned around before walking out and spoke, "I'm not the one to blame here. I didn't do anything wrong."

After getting in the car, Marlo stared at me before turning the car on.

"What?"

"That was fucked up what you did. I want you to know that."

"It was fucked up what I did? What about her? Are you taking her side now?"

"It ain't about that, Sugar. That was some hurtful shit you said to her, and of all days you pick this one."

"She picked the fight with me. Was I supposed to sit there quiet while she reamed me out?"

"I asked you if you wanted to leave."

"Why should I have to run away from her? They were my parents too, and I shouldn't have to leave because of her."

"The time was just not appropriate for that. Now all of your family is looking at you sideways!"

"I don't care about them. They never cared about me when my mother was there whipping my ass for shit that Mya did. Or when they were buying drugs and not feeding us. Fuck them. I'm tired of taking the blame for her. I was abused damn near every night because she wanted to go out and get fucked. Well, it's time she took responsibility for something."

"Look, I understand you being upset, but it still wasn't the place and time for that."

"Well, maybe you're right, but I would have never went off like that if she wouldn't have kept fucking with me."

"Well, let's just go home and chill. You got me now, and I'm going to make it better. I got something that will clear your mind."

"Oh, really?" I said, smiling even though I was still angry about what had just happened.

"Yeah, you know I do," he said as he licked his lips.

Once we entered the hous,e Marlo palmed my ass with both of his hands and begin to kiss me on the back of my neck. I leaned my head to the side as I began to play with my hardened nipples through my shirt. I turned around to face him as stuck my tongue in his mouth as he began to remove my shirt and bra. Once he succeeded he began to play with my nipples with his fingers as we continued to tongue each other down. I reached down and loosened his belt and unbuttoned his pants. After his pants hit the floor I put my hands on his hardness and after removing the pre-cum with my fingers I backed away and licked it off of each finger. Marlo, extremely turned on, stepped out of his pants and began to massage his pole as I removed the remainder of my clothing.

"Come fuck me," I instructed in a sexy tone.

Marlo moved toward me as I backed up and sat on the edge of the chaise. I bent one leg up and began to massage my clit, waiting for him to meet me. He moved closer to me and stuck his stick in my wide open mouth as I continued to play with me clit. I took him all in as he guided my head with his hands. After he was satisfied, he pushed my legs back and entered me, going deep inside of me. He continued to pound me until we both exploded. Exhausted, we fell asleep on the floor wrapped in each other's arms. My mind was definitely off of Mya and the earlier incident. **Though my relationship with Mya was in ruins,** I could move on knowing that I once tried to mend our broken relationship.

Chapter 10

Sugar Walls . . .

I came up with the idea to call my club Sugar Walls after listing to Jackie-O's CD. Though my name was Sugar, the meaning of the song fit the scheme perfectly. I sat down with my designer Noelle and explained what I wanted. And once I decided on a building, the contractors began working. The floors were glazed marble, and the Sugar Walls sign lighted the entrance hall. There would be two booths where the bouncers would sit with the pay station directly in the center. Once inside the main room, there would be four side stages with one main center stage, each equipped with a pole in the middle. The lighting would surround each stage perfectly to spotlight the dancers when they performed. The black tables that would surround the entire room would be covered with crisp, white tablecloths and imported centerpieces. The DJ's booth would be close to the bar , which would feature three bartenders to take food and drink orders from waitresses.

Upstairs would be the two VIP rooms for big ballers and

celebrities with a private bar and a private dancing room in each one. The last two rooms would be for peep shows, where customers could pay to see private themed dances on the opposite side of glass. Each room would have four stations total. The color scheme would be red, black, and white, and the art would be a collection of exotic women in different poses in different places.

During the construction of the building I went to Kinko's to have flyers made to advertise the grand opening. I also posted flyers for an interview day. The open positions were for two cooks, three bartenders, one DJ, four bouncers, two cashiers, three waitresses, two for cleaning, and a minimum of twelve dancers. I also needed a manager and an accountant to keep things running smoothly. I set up a pay scale where the dancers would have to pay me fifteen percent of their earnings. I designed uniforms for all the waitresses, which were similar to a naughty maid's outfit. I was excited about my interviews at the end of the week, and I was surprised when the line formed, wrapping around the corner. I called Marlo in for some assistance with picking the dancers and waitresses.

The first dancer that I chose went by the stage name Chocolate. Born and raised in North Philly, she possessed a gift of consuming your attention. Her smooth, dark skin was perfect, and her body was shaped like a Coke bottle. Her dancing style was graceful but sexy at the same time. She would definitely be a headliner, and Marlo agreed with me. Next was Kitten, who was from Baltimore. Her complexion was caramel, and her 40 DD's made her a sure winner. She had long, glowing legs and she demonstrated how they could wrap around the pole. I automatically put her on the headliner list as well. Diamond was a beauty with golden brown skin. She was the girl next door who could be a runway model. I was mesmerized by her beauty and agreed to make her the third headliner. Brooklyn was the final headliner I chose, and well worth the title. She had a backside that the men would go crazy over at first sight. Her dancing and her booty shaking demonstration won me over within the first few seconds.

Marlo had four of his workers come to be bouncers, and after a long day I had eight peep show girls with names ranging from Vixen to Peaches. The waitresses were Mina, Tressa, and Lexi—three bombshells. The bartenders were all women as well. The cooks were the hardest to find, but with the help of Marlo, I was able to find two excellent cooks that could fix any upscale meal. The DJ, Razor, was a neighborhood dude that played at all of the hood parties, and I chose him because his style was unique. The cashiers and cleaning staff were held off until the following day when I searched for a manager and an accountant. In a matter of two days I had found and hired each person to complete the business.

It was two weeks before the construction was complete, and after filing the necessary papers and passing inspection, the club was ready to open. I had the place decorated for the grand opening, and I went and picked out the perfect outfit to match my decor. In total, Marlo had given me over $100,000 to complete the club, and it was well worth it. Basically, he came in as a silent partner. I was grateful for the help, and I was surely going to prove to him that his money was well spent. His investment was going to make us both rich. I was determined to make sure his money didn't go to waste, and I was just as determined to be on top.

Opening night was more intense than I expected. I had knots in my stomach as Marlo assured me that I had nothing to worry about. I kissed him as I cut the ribbon and opened the door, allowing the first customer to enter. The customers—both male and female—began to crowd the main room where both Chocolate and Kitten were already dancing. Jenna came down to support me, as well as Marissa, whom I hadn't seen in such a long time. I was surprised when she showed up, and we hugged for about a minute before letting go. High rollers stopped in as well and purchased bottles of Dom and Cristal to gain entry to the VIP rooms.

I walked around and greeted most of the customers, and after one walkthrough, I heard a male voice call my name.

"Sugar, Sugar, Sugar. Damn, you look good."

"What the hell are you doing here, JT?"

"I'm here as a customer just like everyone else. I see that nigga is treating you well."

"Yeah, he is, as a matter of fact."

"That's good. Milk is doing your body damn good too. You should come holla at me. I know that you're a big time club owner now and don't need a nigga, but we were good together once."

"Thanks, but no thanks, JT. I'm extremely happy with the man I've got, and you're right, I am a big time club owner and I don't need a nigga!"

"That never stopped you before," he said, moving closer to me.

"Well that was then and this is now! I would have never gotten this far if I would have stayed with your tired ass!" I said, backing away. "I have to get back to work now. I hope that you enjoy yourself."

"I'll be seeing you again, trust me" he said before turning and walking away.

I was annoyed that he would have the audacity to show

his face in my club after the shit that he did to me. Just being in the same room with him made me uncomfortable, but I couldn't allow him to ruin my night.

I went to the ladies' room to get myself together. I stood in front of the mirror for a few minutes, thinking back to that night at the club when JT and Dollar embarrassed the hell out of me. Neither of them would ever have that opportunity again, nor would anyone else. After leaving the ladies' room I noticed Marlo at the bar talking with JT. *What the fuck is he trying to pull?* I quickly went over and interrupted.

"Oh, hey, baby. I'm just here chatting with your old friend."

"He's hardly that!"

"Well, nice talking to you, man. I'll see you around," JT said, shaking Marlo's hand before walking away.

"What was he talking about?" I asked.

"He was just telling me that he's a party promoter. I was just trying to see what he was getting at."

"He's trouble. He played me out with Top Dollar!"

"I know and I don't trust niggas like that. I'm wondering what he has planned, popping up and talking to me and shit."

"I don't know, but I don't trust him either."

"Well, don't let him ruin your night. You have better things to do than worry about him."

"I know," I said, before he kissed me on the forehead.

After walking away I still thought about JT, but I pushed it into the back of my mind as I greeted more customers. I entered the VIP room and noticed Domino in the back. Domino was a high roller who all the women wanted a piece of. As I made my way over to where he was seated, I noticed the look that he gave which was similar to the way a dog looks at a piece of meat. I walked past his group of friends and he smiled when I got close.

"Hey, Domino. Are you having a good time?" I asked.

"I'm having a hell of a time. I didn't know women this fine even lived in Philly. Where the hell did you find them?"

"They found me, and I'm glad you like them."

"Yeah, it's a shame I can't get a lap dance from you," he said, grinning. "I'm just joking. I really would like a lot more from you, but I know you got a man and all, so that's out of the question."

"Yeah, I guess so. Well, let me know if there's anything that I can do for you."

"You know what you could do for me, but I know your all in love and shit, so I'll keep it to myself."

"Well, I appreciate the secrecy."

"Oh it's not a secret at all. I want a piece of you, but your man is cool peeps."

"Well, I have to get back to work, but let me know if they don't give you your money's worth."

"I sure will," he said, licking his lips.

I left the VIP room and went back down to the main area. It was almost time for closing, and the night had been great overall. The club made almost $10,000 at the end of the night, and as each customer left, they let me know how much they enjoyed themselves. I was exhausted once we left, and I fell to sleep within seconds of my head hitting the pillow. Marlo was still out working while I slept and was still out in the morning when I finally woke up. I had grown used to the long nights, but I figured that they would grow longer if he continued to help me with the club. I just hoped that with the money the club was bring-ing in he would be able to back away from the drugs completely and spend more time with me. I hated the fact that he sold drugs, but I knew that without it, I wouldn't be where I was.

Over the next few months the club business was bringing in a lot of money, and the exhaustion that came with it was paying off. I was confident going in that it would do well—just not as good as it had been. We were bringing in over $10,000 a night.

My relationship with Marlo was great except the many calls that he received from Mya which drove me crazy. She always had an excuse for getting him over to her apartment, especially when she heard of the club and grew even more jealous. I knew her calls were just a ploy to get him back, but he ensured me that she would never have the opportunity to get close to him again.

Marissa began to hang out at the club with me a lot, and once she noticed the amount of money the dancers made, she asked me if she could work there. I was a little hesitant at first, but I gave in after she begged me to give her a shot. Instead of letting her be a premiere dancer, I let her dance in the peep show booths so she wouldn't have to worry about the men groping her. She was excited, and after I got her a full makeover, I was too. I never expected Marissa to look as beautiful as she did.

On her first night she was extremely nervous, but I told her she wouldn't be able to see the person on the other side of the glass. While she would dance, she would only see a reflection of herself in a mirror, but the man on the other side would see her. Not all of the peep show booths had the one-way windows, but if the women were a little afraid of being stared at, I put them in those.

I stood in the back of the peep show room as man after man paid for girls. I hinted to the men that Marissa's booth was the one to check out, and soon they were all heading her way. Once the music began playing, she began dancing, and I stood there in awe as she moved like a professional. It appeared that she had been doing this for a long time, and I wished that she'd been working for me from day one.

The club had made a splash on the city, and I was extremely proud of myself. I already knew **Sugar Walls** would make me a rich woman some day.

Chapter 11

A Game of Domino

Domino was one of the most wealthy and feared drug lords in Philadelphia. I met him while working for Dyna advertising the escort service. I wasn't surprised when he started frequenting the club, since most of the drug distributors did. I also wasn't surprised that he continued to get in snide remarks whenever Marlo wasn't around. I wasn't uncomfortable with him. In fact, I was kind of enjoying it. He understood that I was in a relationship and the flirting could be no more than that.

It was Saturday, which was the busiest night of the week. Marlo was out taking care of business, and I was doing my usual round of greeting the customers. After entering the VIP lounge I noticed Domino receiving a lap dance from Diamond. I wasn't going to interrupt, but he quickly dismissed her when he noticed me turning to leave the room.

"Sugar, don't leave. We were just finishing up here," he yelled before motioning me to come closer.

"What's up? Enjoying yourself?"

"Always! Have a seat," he said, patting the cushion next to him.

"I'm working, Domino."

"Well, isn't taking care of your customers part of the job?"

"Yeah it is, but—"

"Well then you should sit down and chat with me."

"Just for a minute," I said, before sitting down.

"You know you're looking fine as hell since you switched back over from clits to dick!" he said, laughing.

"Oh, really? Who said I didn't still like clits!" For some reason his comments didn't annoy me. I had come to know Domino to be a jokester, and I kind of always brushed what he said off as a joke.

"Oh, my bad. But you know dick is much better, especially mine!" he said, grabbing his crotch.

"Domino, you know I can't get with you like that. Marlo is real important to me, and I'm not trying to lose him," I replied, trying to make it clear that I didn't have any intention of cheating on Marlo.

"I know that, since you make sure you tell me that every time I approach you. I'm just trying to have some fun, that's all. I'm not trying to fuck up your relationship with him at all. I told you he was cool peeps."

"I'm trying to be faithful to him, my relationships in the past have been crazy, and this one is working, so I'm going to do my best to keep it going."

"I know you don't think he's faithful to you. You can't possibly think he doesn't still tap your sister when he gets a chance to or any other chick, for that matter."

"I do believe that. I trust him."

"That much trust is going to leave you with a broken heart. You can't trust a man to be faithful. We ain't built like that."

"Well, unless it's proven otherwise, I believe that he's faithful."

"You'll get proof, trust me, and when you do, I'll be here to make you feel better."

"Domino, I'm sure you know that breaking another man's character won't make you win in the end. Next time try pumping yourself up. You may get a batter reaction. Now, I have to get back to work. You enjoy yourself, OK?"

"OK, but remember what I said."

"I will, and you remember what I said. It might help you score well with a real woman one day," I said, getting up from the chair.

I was a little bothered by his insinuation of Marlo's infidelity, especially with Mya. I could deal with him screwing any other chick but her because I knew at the end of the night I was number one. I had learned that men cheat, and either you can deal with it or move on. I'd rather deal with the one I had then move on to a whole different situation that would only cause me more aggravation. Men were all pretty much the same.

I tried to forget what Domino said, but I would definitely pay more attention to Marlo's outings, if only to prove him wrong. I went down to the bar and had a drink, and as I sipped it I took in my surroundings. The club was packed as usual, and Chocolate was on the stage performing. While the men were going crazy over her gliding down the pole, I sat on the stool and watched as thoughts of Marlo ran through my mind. Overall our relationship had been great, and I had no reason to doubt his feelings for me this time, since he'd worked hard to show me how true they really were. For the first time I was in a relationship that kept me happy and I was enjoying every minute of it.

Marlo decided to show his face around 1:30AM, when

the club was a half hour away from closing. I was annoyed that he hadn't shown up all night, and I made sure that he knew it as soon as he made it inside the office and closed the door behind him.

"Where the hell have you been?" I yelled.

"Handling business like I told you. What's your problem? And since when did you start questioning me about where I've been?"

"Since now! I've been thinking about the fact that you spend a lot of time *handling business* instead of spending time with me."

"Handling business is what got you this club."

"Are you still fucking with Mya?" I asked.

"Where the hell did that come from?"

"I asked you a question, Marlo!"

"No, I'm not. Did she tell you that?"

"No, I just wanted to know."

"I don't know what happened since we left home earlier today, but you're tripping right now."

"I'm not tripping. Your behavior just seems suspicious."

"My behavior? What behavior? I've been the same way since you got with me."

"I'm just not trying to get hurt, that's all."

"I told you before that I'm not going to hurt you, and I meant that."

"Well, I'm sorry for snapping on you. I was just worried, OK?"

"All right, well don't make it a habit," he said, coming over to kiss me.

"I'm going down to make sure the workers are getting ready to close."

"All right, thanks. I'll be down in a minute."

"All right," he said, before leaving the office.

I was angry with myself for believing what Domino said.

I should have went with my heart and believed that Marlo was honest with me. I counted the earnings for the night and locked it up in the safe. Before leaving the room I promised myself to always follow my heart and not let other people influence me to go another way.

After closing, Marlo and I went home, and since I flipped out on him at the club earlier, I felt that it would only be right if I made it up to him. After he showered I was waiting for him on the bed, naked and already massaging my clit with my fingers. He stood there staring at me, and I continued to play with myself and moan loudly. He was at attention within a few seconds and making his way over to the bed. He moved my hand out of the way to make room for his tongue, and I was delighted with the warmness of his contact.

"Damn, that feels good," I moaned before placing my hand on the back of his head.

He continued to satisfy me until I exploded and he sucked the juices from me. He stood up and pulled me down to the edge of the bed. After gently rubbing my clit with the tip of his pole, he pushed it deep inside of me. His circular motions were sending me into orgasm after orgasm. I began to scream, "I love you!" over and over again while digging my nails into his back. It wasn't long before he erupted inside of me. I closed my eyes shortly after that and fell asleep in his arms.

The next morning I noticed that I had a missed call and a voicemail on my phone. I didn't recognize the number, but as soon as the message played, I knew the voice and it made my skin crawl.

"Hey, baby, I miss you. I know you're wondering how I got the number, but that doesn't really matter. I'm trying to see you soon. I got some information about that dude you're fucking with that might be beneficial to you. When

you get a chance holla at me, one!" JT said, ending the
message before the beep.

Who the hell gave him my number? It had been changed at
least twice since we broke up. I wondered what information could he possibly have that would be beneficial to me
about Marlo. I wasn't sure where all of these accusations
were coming from, and I was going to find out one way or
another. I didn't trust JT, so I wasn't going to call him, but
I would get in contact with Domino. I knew that Marlo was
in and out of the club, so I couldn't talk to him there. I
had to find out where he hung out at during the day.

Once Marlo left home I dialed Jenna, because if anyone
knew where to find him, it was her. She answered the
phone on the third ring.

"What's up, Sugar?" Jenna asked.

"You know that dude Domino, right?"

"Do I know him? Who doesn't know him? What about
him?"

"Do you know where he hangs at?"

"He doesn't really stay in one spot, but you know that
apartment complex across from that bar in Darby we used
to go to all the time?"

"Yeah, I remember."

"Well it's this store behind it that he owns. He's in there
some time, and if not, I'm sure that they can get in contact
with him for you."

"OK cool, thanks."

"Why do you need to get with him?"

"I've been having suspicions about Marlo, and Domino
is just one of the people throwing salt in the game. I don't
trust the other person that told me something, so I need
to find Domino to find out exactly what it is that he knows
about him."

"How can you trust him? You don't know him like that."

"I know, but I need to find out what everyone is talking about."

"Well I know how you feel, but be careful because he's a dude that's out for self."

"I will, and thanks for the information."

"You're welcome," she said before we ended the call.

I got dressed and left the house, making the drive to find Mr. Domino. Once I reached the store I noticed a group of guys on the opposite side of the street. I got out of the car and went into the store and walked up to the register.

"How can I help you, pretty lady?" the cashier spoke while looking me up and down.

"I'm trying to locate Domino."

"Why?"

"Because I need to ask him something," I replied.

"Well, I can't help you."

"Look, if you call him I'm sure he'll want to talk to me."

"Ms. Sugar, what brings you all the way to this part of town?" a voice spoke from behind.

Turning around noticing Domino standing at the door, I said, "You!"

"Oh, you know her boss? I thought she was 5-0," the cashier said.

"No, she's cool," Domino informed him. "So you were looking for me?"

"Yes, I was. I need to get some information from you."

"I assume it's about your man."

"That's right."

"Well let's go upstairs and we can talk."

"OK," I said, following him out of the store to the door that led to an upstairs apartment. After entering the apartment I sat down on one of the chairs in the living room.

"So what is it that you need to know?"

"I need to know what he's doing and who he's doing it with."

"And you think that I am the man that can help you with that?"

"You told me that I would find out that he wasn't faithful to me, and you must know something if you said that."

"Yeah, I do know something, but I didn't say that I would rat him out. I ain't no rat, ma."

"Well then I'll be leaving if you can't help me," I said, standing up from the seat.

"I didn't say that I wouldn't help you. I said that I wouldn't rat him out that's all."

"So how can you possibly help me without ratting him out?"

"I can give you the information you need to find the information on your own."

"Oh, really? How is that?"

"Look it's not hard to do if you check his whereabouts. Check up on him when he tells you where he's going. Check out how much time he spends at your sister's spot. Things like that will give you all you need to know."

"Well thanks, but I already know that."

"Well look, I'm sorry that I can't be of more assistance, but I'm not a snitch, baby. I'm glad that you came to see me, though. I wish it was on different terms," he said, licking his lips.

"Well, I thought you were going to help me out. I already told you that I wouldn't believe that he was cheating unless I had proof, and I still don't have that."

"You already doubt that he's faithful or you wouldn't be here asking me questions about him."

"That's not true."

"Yeah, just like it's not true that you want me," he said, moving close to me.

"That's not true!" I said, backing away.

"I bet your panties are wet right now."

"Look, I have to go," I said, moving toward the door.

"Well, you know where to find me when you're ready."

"Good-bye, Domino," I said after opening the door.

I made my way out to the car angry that I had driven all the way down there for nothing. I knew that if I was going to find out anything about Marlo I would have to look myself. I decided that I would begin my research that night.

Once the club opened, Marlo stayed for about the first hour and a half before leaving as usual. As soon as he left, I told Tina my manager that I would make a quick run. I borrowed Tina's car to avoid him noticing me and followed Marlo closely. His first stop was to one of the houses where his workers held the product. He stayed in there about fifteen minutes before returning to his car. The next stop was none other than Mya's, and I was pissed. Domino was right, and I felt like an asshole for believing Marlo's lie. He didn't even knock on the door; instead, he used a key. I sat in the car for about a half hour before going back to the club. I didn't need any more proof since he had no reason to be at her place at 1:00 in the morning, nor did he need a key unless there was something going on.

After I entered the club you could see the anger on my face. I was on my way into the office when I ran into Domino coming out of the VIP lounge.

"What's up, ma? You all right?"

"Yeah, I'm fine," I said opening the door.

"You don't look OK."

"I said I'm fine!"

"All right then, I'm out. I'll see you around."

I went into the office and slammed the door. I screamed in anger because I trusted Marlo and he lied to me. I sat down in the chair and tears began to flow. I had believed in our relationship and though it started on forbidden terms, I never thought he would cheat on me with her. I knew that he still had feelings for her, but with all of her betrayal I thought that he was finished with her for sure. After the club closed I called his cell phone and he didn't pick up. I began driving, not sure where I was headed, but I knew that I wasn't ready to go home quite yet.

I drove around with the windows down while I cried. I knew that I needed someone to talk to. I decided to go to Jenna's place but she wasn't home. I sat in the car outside of her apartment for about twenty minutes, hoping she would come home to keep me from going to a place I knew I shouldn't go. When she didn't show I made the drive down to Domino's store since I didn't know where he lived. Of course the store was closed, but I did see a light on in the upstairs apartment. I got out of the car and rang the bell. A few minutes later a tall, slim guy with a do rag tied around his head answered the door.

"What's up, who are you?" he asked.

"My name is Sugar. Is Domino here?"

"If you knew him like that, you would know that he doesn't live here."

"Well I know that you don't know me, so I wouldn't expect you to tell me where he lives, but if you could give him my number and ask him to call me, I would appreciate it," I said, passing him my business card.

"Yeah, I can do that."

"Thanks," I said walking away.

I got in the car and began to drive away and my cell phone began ringing. I answered it on the first ring.

"Hello."

"Looking for me again?" Domino asked.

"Yeah, I needed someone to talk to."

"Well I'm on my way home now if you want to meet me there."

"I just want to talk, OK?"

"I heard you the first time, ma. Do you want to come over or not?" he said, annoyed.

"Yeah, I do."

He gave me the address and the directions to the house. I was nervous as I pulled up in his driveway in back of his Denali truck. I got out of my car and walked toward the door and he opened it before I got a chance to knock.

"I see you didn't get lost," he said, smiling.

I stood there for a second, looking him up and down before stepping into the house. I never really looked at how fine he was until now. I never really paid as much attention to his looks as I did his comments. He stood about six feet with a muscular build. His skin was smooth and free of blemish. His hair was jet black with waves like the waters of Miami Beach. His lounging pants showed the print of his manhood and turned me on instantly. I looked away when he noticed me staring down below and smiled. After entering the house we walked into the living room and sat down on the sofa in front of the 52-inch plasma TV.

"So what's up? What did you want to talk about?" he asked.

"I followed Marlo tonight," I said, looking down at the floor.

"Oh, really? I guess that you found out something and that's why you snapped when I saw you earlier."

"Yeah, I did, and I'm sorry for snapping on you. I was just angry."

"Well, what did you find out?"

"I saw him going into Mya's apartment, and with a key at that!"

"Well I hate to say I told you so, but you can't trust that a man won't cheat. I told you that."

"So what about you, do you have a girl?" I asked, since I didn't want her to walk in and find me sitting there. I'd had enough drama for one night.

"Yeah, I do."

"Well where is she now?"

"She's home. She doesn't live here. I have multiple homes."

"Well she won't be coming over here tonight, will she?"

"No, she won't. Why?"

"Because I might be staying if you make me feel better."

I was frustrated with Marlo and hurt. I needed comfort, and I knew that having sex with another man was the wrong way to do it, but hell, he was cheating on me with Mya. I didn't care about saving his feelings since he obviously didn't care about saving mine.

"I'm a professional at making women feel good."

"Well prove it to me," I instructed without a second thought.

"Are you positive that you want me to do that?"

Instead of speaking, I began to unbutton my dress and that was his cue. I knew that I was wrong for trying to get back at Marlo, but I needed to be taken care of right then, and Domino was the man to make that happen. His touch instantly sent chills up my spine, and my body shook as he moved closer to me and kissed my neck. I wanted to stop him right at that moment and run out of the house, but I couldn't because his touch was making me weak. I would have never believed that a drug lord could be this gentle with a woman. From what I'd always heard about drug dealers or saw on TV, in their element there were ruthless. I guess being around a woman brings out the gentle side.

I closed my eyes as he continued to remove the remainder of my clothing. I was anticipating his next move because each one felt better than the previous. Soon I was bent over the sofa with his hands around my waist and him pounding me from behind. He continued to hit my G-spot from the back until he pulled out to change positions. He sat on the chair and instructed me to get on top, and I followed his direction. I straddled him and moved my hips to grind into him. He grabbed my breasts as I moved up and down and in slow circles until he grabbed hold of me to stop.

"Damn, your going to make me cum too quick," he spoke, still holding onto me to restrict my movement. Once he let go I continued the motion that was interrupted before. I picked up the pace as I neared an orgasm, and once I reached it, the trembling of my body and the contracting of my walls caused him to erupt as well. We sat there staring at each other speechless and exhausted.

"Are you OK?" he asked.

"I'm good."

"You're not feeling guilty, are you?"

"No. Why should I feel guilty when he did the same thing to me?"

"I'm just checking. You want to go up and get a shower?"

"Yeah, we can do that."

"We?"

"Yeah, if you're up for round two."

"Oh, I'm up for it!" he said, smiling.

We went upstairs and showered and continued with our second round of sex. After getting out of the shower we got into his king-sized bed and fell to sleep.

After waking up in the morning I noticed that I had four voicemails that I figured were from Marlo. I decided not to listen to them, and after getting dressed I said good-bye to Domino and made my way home.

I did feel a little bit of guilt after leaving, but it wasn't enough to keep me from seeing him. It became an addiction, and I didn't know how to free myself from it. Marlo kept seeing Mya and I was sure of it because I still followed him from time to time, not letting him know that I was on to him. Instead, I kept the information in my back pocket until I needed it. **The game that I was playing with Domino** was the only thing keeping Marlo and me together, though we were only hanging on by strings.

I began spending most of my nights with Domino for the next three months, since Marlo wasn't interested in any of my time. My life was beginning to mirror the way it was when I was with JT. I found that it was a pattern for me. When I was in a relationship that was going bad, I immediately looked for companionship somewhere else. I hated that my relationships had all turned bad. I envied the people on television with perfect marriages and relationships, and I dreamed that I would accomplish the same things.

After a long night at the club, Domino had planned to cook dinner for me, and I was excited since I had never dealt with anyone that would take the time to cook me a meal. I drove over to his house, and after he greeted me, I went up and took a quick shower before meeting him at the table. I smiled when I saw the feast that he had prepared. I sat down as he pulled out a chair for me.

"I can't believe that you cooked all of this for me."

"Well believe it, baby. I'm full of surprises."

"I can see that."

"I want to take you on a trip, but I know you're probably scared to leave your man."

"That might be a possibility. I have to see how things go."

"That's fair enough."

"Well, this food looks amazing. I'm interested in sampling it."

"Well get to it, baby!" he said, smiling.

After eating we went up to the bedroom where our night ended with a round of sex. I thought about going away with him, and the sound of it enticed me. I wanted to be more daring, and this would be a way to clear my head for a few days anyway. When Domino asked me where I wanted to go, I told him that since I had never been out of Pennsylvania before anywhere would be a vacation for me. He couldn't believe that I hadn't been anywhere, but I briefed him on my past so that he could better understand all that I had been through.

The more time I spent with Domino, the more I began to care about him. I never expected to want anything more than sex from him. He was just supposed to occupy my time. I knew that I couldn't leave Marlo because the business would get sticky, but I knew that I couldn't just sit home and know that he was out screwing Mya while I sat home alone. The mind was unpredictable, and I could have never known what it would do with my relationship. I began gathering the clothing and accessories I needed for our four-day trip. I nervous when we left because I lied to Marlo by telling him I was going away with Marissa. I had to pay her to stay home from work while I was gone. I prayed that he wouldn't run into her anywhere while I was away. Our destination was Las Vegas, and though I had seen views on TV, I could have never imagined how beautiful it would be. We drove from the airport to the hotel so we could get changed and head for the casinos.

"I am so excited. I can't believe that we are really here."

"Believe it, baby, and as soon as you're mine, there will be a lot more to come."

I sat silent because my feelings for Marlo were too strong to walk away right now. I cared about Domino, but I wasn't certain that his feelings were sincere.

"Why the silent treatment now? Did I say something wrong?" he asked.

"No, I'm just not sure what I want to do."

"You know that he's cheating with your sister, that should be enough."

"I know, but I love him, and I believe that he loves me too."

"That's not love, and hopefully one day you'll figure it out. I'm not going to say that I'm the most honest and loving person in the world, but I know the difference. I know when you love someone and when you don't. I'm not a bullshitter. That dude is a liar, and he doesn't love you."

"Why don't we just enjoy this vacation and each other? While we're here we can worry about us and worry about the rest of that when we get back. Is that cool?"

"That's fine with me baby."

I enjoyed the remainder of those days in Las Vegas, so much so that I didn't want to go back home. It was like a dream that I didn't want to wake up from. Once we arrived back home, I knew things had to change. I knew I needed to make some decisions if I was going to be happy, and freeing myself from Marlo was at the top of my list.

Chapter 12

Tear us apart

Iknew it wouldn't be long before I would be forced to confront Marlo with what I knew about him and Mya. I had also found out the information that JT was speaking of when he called me on the phone that day. Domino and I began to creep for the next two months on a regular basis. Marlo was a major figure, so I knew that sooner or later someone would see us together and notify Marlo. I was just getting in from the club and was surprised to find Marlo home. I expected him to be out at Mya's. I put down my purse and walked into the living room where he was watching TV.

"Surprised to see you here," I said, sitting down on the chair to remove my shoes.

"I'm surprised to see you too. Thought you'd be out with Domino!" he spat.

"What?"

"I guess you thought I wouldn't find out. Well guess what? I did!"

"You don't know what you're talking about, Marlo!"

"Oh, I know what I'm talking about. I know that all of those mornings that I came home to an empty bed you were sleeping with him."

"Who told you that?"

"It doesn't matter who told me, the point is you are fucking another nigga after all of the shit I've done for you! That's real foul, Sugar."

"Well, I guess we're even then!"

"What the hell do you mean by that?"

"I know you're still fucking Mya. That's the only reason I started messing with Domino in the first place. I followed you to her apartment many nights and watched you use your key to go in!"

"Oh, so you were following me?"

"Yes, I was because people were telling me that you weren't being honest with me so I had to see for myself."

"So what did you see? Me going into my son's mother's place?"

"At 1:00 in the fucking morning, Marlo. The only reason you would have to go over there that late is for some pussy!"

"I'm not fucking her!"

"Well, how the hell did she get pregnant again? Huh?" I asked. "Speechless, huh? I thought so," I said, walking away.

"Sugar!" he yelled. "I didn't know she was pregnant."

"Bullshit, Marlo. If you didn't know, you damn sure should have expected it if you were over there fucking her raw!"

"Sugar, it wasn't even like that."

"Well, what was it? You lied to me, Marlo, and I was hurt. Domino was the only way that I could continue to be with you after I knew what you did." I began to cry. "It hurt like hell to see you going into her apartment. I trusted you."

"I trusted you too, Sugar."

"So it was OK for you to cheat, but it wasn't for me?"

"No it wasn't OK for either one of us to cheat, two wrongs don't make a right, but I know that if I wouldn't have cheated you would have never cheated on me."

"I know that I wouldn't have, but it's too late now."

"It's not too late for us to make it right."

"Marlo, you have a baby on the way. There's no way that we can make things work. I love you with all of my heart, but we've both stepped outside of the relationship."

"That's the reason why we can do this. I don't want to be with her, I need to be with you."

"You told me that before, and twice you went back. I don't know what it is about her that keeps you coming back, but it's obviously something that I'm lacking."

"That's not true. You have everything I want. I don't know why I went back. I can't explain it."

"Well, I can't risk that happening again, and I don't know if I can be with you knowing that you got her pregnant again."

"We don't even know if she's pregnant by me. She could be pregnant by someone else."

"That's true, but I have a strong feeling that it's yours. I'm going up to bed now, but I think we both need time to clear heads."

"Are you saying you're leaving?"

"No, and I'm not asking you to leave either. I'm just saying that we need time to clear our heads, so for now we'll just be roommates until we sort things out."

"Are you serious?"

"Yes."

"I can deal with that, as long as you're not leaving. I still have hope that we'll make it. I promise you that I will let her go."

"Good-night, Marlo!" I said, going upstairs to go to sleep.

That night I felt a little relief that everything was out on the table. I thought about leaving and if I could handle the business on my own, but then I would have to pay him back to buy him out, and I wasn't really trying to give up that kind of money. The true test would be how we could co-exist in the house while not in a committed relationship. I needed him to prove that he would let Mya go before I could drop Domino. I still felt the same way about Marlo as I did in the beginning of the relationship. He had done a lot for me, and I appreciated it, but I couldn't go on believing that he loved me the same. Whatever he and Mya had was stronger ,and though I thought what we had was pretty tight, she was able to **tear us apart**.

The following day I informed Domino of what happened with Marlo. Since we were taking a break from each other, I knew that I could hang out with Domino without the fear of Marlo finding out. Once I hit him with the good news, he told me that he would plan a special night for us, and I was genuinely excited. Once I was dressed and on my way out the door, Marlo came into the house and asked me about where I was heading. I really wasn't in the mood for 101 questions, but I kept my cool.

"Where are you going? Do you have a date or something?"

"Actually I do, how do I look?"

"You know I'm not cool with this, Sugar. This shit ain't right!"

"I know but this is the way that things have to be for a while."

"Well, can I at least get a kiss before you leave?"

"I have to go, Marlo. I'll see you later."

"I'm going to play your little game because I want you

to know how much I want to be with you. Fuck the street shit, I need you back. I'm going to hold off on fucking that nigga up because that still won't make you come back, but just know this shit ain't going to go on for too long."

"Good-night Marlo, don't wait up for me!" I said before walking out of the door.

I knew he was probably upset that I ran out without kissing him, but I knew that if his lips touched mine I wouldn't be able to leave without making love to him. Staying away from him would be one of the hardest things that I ever had to do, but I couldn't allow myself to be second best to Mya anymore. I deserved a hell of a lot more than that!

After entering the restaurant where Domino was waiting for me, I was escorted to the table by the hostess. Domino was looking good enough to eat in his cream linen pantsuit. He stood up to kiss me when I reached the table. I noticed his excitement as he looked me over. I knew that I looked good, and the extra short dress that I was wearing was chosen purposely to entice him and to piss Marlo off at the same time.

"You look good as hell tonight," he said, smiling.

"Thanks, quiet as it's kept you look good as hell too!" I said as I sat down.

"Well thanks, I try, you know," he said, laughing.

"So you know I had to practically pry Marlo off my leg to get out of the house tonight."

"Well, you know dude ain't giving up on you. Shit, I wouldn't give up on you either."

"Domino, I appreciate you being here for me with all of this stuff I'm going through with Marlo. I apologize for using you to piss him off, but I really do like you a lot and I care for you."

"I told you that I would be here for you, and I meant

that. On the real, I don't care if you are trying to make him jealous because I'm enjoying all the time I am spending with you. So I thank him for fucking up, or I wouldn't have gotten the chance to know you."

"Well, it worked out for the both of us!"

"I got a little something for you."

"You can't start spoiling me now. I might fall in love with you," I said, jokingly. Though I knew it was easy for me to fall for someone, I hoped that I could end this before things got that deep.

"That's cool," he said, passing me a long, thin box across the table.

Opening the box, my eyes lit up like the street lights at sun down. The box contained a tennis bracelet with pink diamonds.

"Domino, you shouldn't have done this. This is the most beautiful thing I've even seen." I pulled it out of the box and gave it to him so that he could put it on me. As I sat there with my arm out, I continued to smile. I rose out of my seat a little so that I could kiss him. I wanted to show him how much I appreciated him and everything that he had done for me.

"I can see why that girlfriend of yours is in love with you!" I smiled.

"Yeah, I'm the shit," he said, with a laugh.

We both laughed for a few seconds before stopping. After eating dinner we went over to his place. I entered the house first and as he was locking the door I was stripping off my clothes. By the time he reached the living room I was standing there butt naked. As he entered the room he stood there and stared at me. I used my finger and motioned for him to come over to the chair and sit down. I walked over to the radio and placed my R. Kelly *12 Play* CD that I had brought along into the CD player. I skipped through the CD until reaching "It Seems Like You're Ready."

I had learned a lot from watching the dancers in the club, and I wanted to show off my newly discovered talent. As the song began, "with . . . temperatures rising," I slowly walked over to him and turned around so that my ass was directly in front of his face. I bent over and popped my ass a little and dropped down to the floor in a quick motion. I could feel his excitement as I sat down on the floor, and with my knees bent, I used my hands to help me lift my bottom from the ground in a continuous wave like motion.

As the chorus played over again, I placed my left leg over his right shoulder and moved just close enough for him to kiss my already wet kitty. Domino didn't waste any time savoring the taste of my juices as I began to play with my extremely sensitive nipples. After my first orgasm, I backed up to give him time to free his manhood from his pants and boxers. He sat there and played with it until I got on my knees and met the head with my tongue. The taste of the pre cum excited me even more and I used both hands to stroke his pole as I formed suction around it with my mouth.

"Damn, baby, that shit feels good," he spoke lightly as he laid his head back.

I continued the motion until he came, and I swallowed every drop as I continued to stroke his length until it was at attention again and ready to dwell inside of me. I laid down on the floor as he moved closer to me and slowly rammed his stick inside of my throbbing tunnel. It wasn't long before he was hitting my G-spot, causing orgasm after orgasm. My juices were flowing like the Niagara Falls, and the extra lubrication only excited him more.

He moved in continuous slow circles until he erupted again, and as he moved down to the floor and lay next to me, I knew that it would be much harder than I thought to leave him alone. My feelings for him were growing much too strong to just walk away, and I was truly confused on what I would do, especially since I still loved Marlo.

The following morning I kissed Domino good-bye and drove home. I tried to sneak in the house because I had such a great night with Domino that I didn't really feel like arguing with Marlo about it. I noticed that the light was on in the kitchen, so I made my way in there to say hello.

"Good morning," I said with a slight smile.

"I see you pulled an all-nighter. I didn't know that was part of the plan."

"It wasn't. It just ended up that way."

"I see that nigga's buying you shit now," he said, pointing to my wrist, which was sporting the new bracelet. I had forgotten to remove it before I came home.

"Who said he bought it?"

"Well, you weren't wearing that shit when you left!" he yelled.

"Look, Marlo, I'm going upstairs to get my stuff together for work tomorrow. I'll talk to you later."

"I'm not going to wait on you forever. I'm not the game playing type."

"Oh, really? Well what do you call what you did to me?"

"I wasn't playing. I just got caught up in a situation that I regret."

"Well you should regret it, Marlo. You promised me that you and Mya were through, but that was a damn lie."

"Do you love him?"

"What?"

"I said do you love him? Because if you do and you really want to be with him, I'll let you go."

"No, I don't love him, but I do care for him, and Domino has a girlfriend. We're just hanging out."

"Hanging out? That's what sex is called now?" he said, being sarcastic.

"I'm not going to argue about this right now, Marlo."

"I'm tired of you walking out on me when I want to talk. I have things to say, and you keep walking away," he said, as he tried to grab hold of my arm.

"Because you'll never understand why I feel the way I do, and I'm not ready to explain it," I said, pulling my arm away.

"Well when will you be ready? How long am I supposed to play the background while you go out fucking this nigga?"

"I don't know, I just . . ." I knew that he was frustrated, but I didn't know what else to say.

"That's what I figured you would say!" he said, slamming his plate down on the counter and walking out of the kitchen.

I knew that it was killing him that I was going out with Domino. I didn't enter into this relationship with the intentions of hurting him in any way. I never expected that he would hurt me the way that he did, and in turn force me to hurt him the same. I was sure that I wouldn't be able to keep this up for long, and I knew that I had to make a choice.

As I decided on what outfit I would wear that evening, I decided that I wanted Domino, but first I had to convince him to drop his girl, and I wasn't sure how easy that would be since they had been together for the last three years. I did know that he cared about me, but the test would be how quick he would accept my proposition.

Shay, which was his girlfriend's name, went to the same hair salon that I did. Usually the women of all of the drug distributors went there. I started going there once I got together with Marlo. I didn't find out that Shay was Domino's girl until I already had been dealing with him for a few weeks. By then I didn't care who she was. I already knew that he had a girl the first time we had sex, and it didn't make a difference to me. I had sensed that she knew something was going on between him and I when her hellos soon turned to evil stares. She never approached me about it, but I knew that she had heard about us by the way that she looked at me.

I had and appointment at 3:00 with Tammi, my stylist. I wore my new bracelet purposely in case Shay was in the salon when I arrived. I wouldn't flat out say to anyone that Domino bought it for me, but I wouldn't say that Marlo bought it either, so she would know where I got in from. I entered the salon with a smile on my face after noticing her car parked in the small lot on the side of the building. I waved to everyone showing off my new jewelry.

"Hey, ladies," I said doing a Miss America wave. You could tell that Shay was getting sick to her stomach.

As I reached Tammi's station she looked at me and chuckled.

"Bitch, you know you ain't right!" She reached out to hug me.

"What?" I asked, playing the dumb role.

"Showing off those diamonds, trying to piss her off. Her man bought that, huh?"

"I ain't trying to piss her off," I said, walking to the bench to sit.

"Yeah, right. I'm almost done. I'll be with you in a minute."

Soon Shay's stylist Deena was finished with her hair and she was out the door. I laughed when she gave me one last roll of the eyes before she left. Little did she know her man was soon going to be mine, and I would make sure of that.

After leaving the salon I went home and began to get dressed. It was about 5:00 when I reached home and about 7:00 when I left to go to the club. The doors opened at 9:00, and the men began pouring in shortly after that. I wasn't surprised that Marlo didn't show up because he was probably still angry about the conversation that we had that morning. I did my usual rounds of the club, and I was smiling from ear to ear when I spotted Domino entering the door. I walked over to greet him and he smiled when he noticed me coming in his direction.

"Hey, baby. What's up?" he said, reaching out to hug me.

"I was thinking about you. I wanted to talk to you about something."

"Oh, yeah? What's that?" he asked.

"Walk me up to my office so we can talk," I said, grabbing him by the hand and leading him in the direction of the stairs. After reaching the office and closing the door behind us, I kissed him slowly. He wrapped his arms around me as we tongued each other down for at least a minute.

"So what's up?" he asked, sitting down in the chair.

"I've been thinking about us, and I want us to be together," I said, sitting down on his lap.

"We are together," he replied.

"I mean really together, Dom. I want to be your woman. I'm ready to leave Marlo alone."

"Really? You think you can let that nigga go?"

"I know I can. I'm just not sure if you can let Shay go."

"That ain't nothing, Shay and I been through for a while now."

"Really, why didn't you tell me?"

"Because you didn't ask. That's a done deal. So if you want to be mine that is definitely possible, but you gotta move out of that spot like ASAP. You can't be living in that house with him and be my woman."

"That's cool, but I don't have anywhere to go right now. I can get an apartment, but I really don't have time to go out looking, and I don't want to just settle for anything just for a quick move."

I could have gotten my own place, but I needed to be closer to him to watch his actions. If I would have moved into my own place, he would never have to come home to me. Though he had more than one house, I planned on getting him to stay with me. That was the only way I could see things working.

"All of the homes I have, you know you have somewhere to go."

"I'm ready. I mean it from the bottom of my heart. I want us to be together."

"Well, then it's done! Meet me at the house tomorrow with your things, and then we can move on with this."

"I will, Dom, I promise," I said, kissing him.

"Girl, you lucky you have a business to run, or I would have you bent over this desk," he said, grabbing his crotch.

"Well, lock the door baby and bend me over," I said seductively.

He rose up out of the chair and went to lock the door, and soon I was bent over the desk with him ramming me from behind and it felt so damn good. I moaned as he hit the right spots in his circular motions. The loud music that played in the club intensified the sex, and I pushed my ass back harder as he went as deep inside of me as he could go. I let out a loud scream as we both reached our orgasms in sync.

"That was good as hell, baby," he said before going into my office bathroom to clean up.

"Good ain't the word for it," I said, laughing.

Once he was done I went into the bathroom and cleaned up and we both walked out of the office smiling. I continued my night as usual, and after leaving the club, I went home and started to pack my things while Marlo was out of the house. When I woke up in the morning, I loaded everything into the back of my car and headed for Domino's. I left Marlo, not explaining what I had decided, and I was on my way to a new life with a new man.

Chapter 13

Short Lived . . .

It had been five months since the day I walked out on Marlo and moved in with Domino to pursue a full-fledged relationship. Though Marlo tried to rekindle the first few weeks, he soon gave up when he realized that I wasn't coming back. Shay still continued to give me the evil eye when she would see me in the salon, but I gave it right back to her each time. Domino's warnings were the only thing keeping me from whipping her ass. Sugar Walls was still thriving, and I had saved at least $70,000. My bank account was full and my relationship with Domino was better than I could have ever imagined it would be.

Domino's birthday was coming, and I had planned to host a birthday party for him at the club. I hired a premier party planner and explained my ideas. I chose everything from the color scheme to the napkins that would lace the tables. I designed the perfect outfit and had it tailor-made.

I was excited the night of the party, and each detail was playing out perfectly. After I was dressed and on my way to the club, I called Domino on his cell to make sure that he would be there on time.

"Hey, baby. What's up?" he asked.

"Where are you?"

"Tying up some loose ends. Why what's up?"

"I'm on my way to the club now. You are supposed to be there by ten. Don't be late, OK?"

"I'm not going to be late. When I'm done here I'm going to get dressed and be on my way."

"All right."

"So, I'll see you when I get there."

"OK."

I had put a lot of time and money into this party, and I didn't want to look like a fool if he showed up late or not at all. I opened the doors at nine, and it was packed within the first half hour. I was smiling from ear to ear when my man arrived on time, looking as good as a well-done piece of prime rib. He wore a cream linen pantsuit and shoes. His hair was freshly cut and he smiled when he noticed how good I looked in my custom designed attire. I could see all of the envy when he walked up to me and kissed me before ever greeting any of his guests. His attempt at making me feel like a queen was definitely working. He looked me up and down and smiled as I turned around, allowing him to view my outfit from all angles.

"This is real nice, baby. I really appreciate this."

"Well, I'm glad that I can make you happy! Now go and greet your guests since they are all waiting to see you."

"Cool, don't go too far," he said, smiling.

"I won't."

I walked in the direction of the bar. I watched him as he greeted people individually. Each person was excited, waiting for their turn to shake hands with "the man." It wasn't long before I decided to get out on the floor and dance as the DJ began to play the songs I had selected. Domino stood and watched me as I danced alone. I shook each body part a little harder when I took notice to his stares. It wasn't long before he joined me on the floor and began to dance so close to me that we could have been one.

After dancing two songs straight, I let him continue enjoying his guests. As I headed to the ladies room, I noticed Shay entering the door. I instantly stopped in my tracks and changed my direction. There was no way that I was going to allow her to ruin this night for me. I had planned each detail to the letter, and she definitely had no place in it. As she made her was through the crowd in Domino's direction, I pushed through the crowds of people to stop her. As soon as she reached the spot where he was standing, she tapped him on the shoulder and as he turned around. He seemed happy that she had showed up. If this were a cartoon this would be the scene where the smoke began to come out of my ears because I was fuming mad. He gave her a hug and then quickly let go when he noticed that I was a few steps away.

"What the hell are you doing here? You weren't invited!" I screamed with my hand pressed against my hip.

"Actually I was invited, wasn't I, Dom?"

"Yeah, I invited her," he stated, looking at my disgusted expression.

"Why the hell would you do that?" I asked, getting even more upset.

"Because she's a good friend of mine."

"Oh, really?"

"Look, Sugar. It's my birthday, and I don't want to argue about this."

"We don't have to, just ask her to leave."

"I'm not going to do that," he spoke before sipping his drink.

"Fine! Have a great fucking time!" I yelled before heading to my office.

I sat there pondering my next move. I was pissed that he had the nerve to invite his ex into my club. He was definitely going to be sorry for that. I wasn't about to let that slide. I looked out of my office widow and could see the two of them on the dance floor, smiling and laughing. Instead of displaying any more of my anger to the two of them, I went back out to the party and acted as if their show of affection wasn't bothering me one bit. The party was almost over and I faked it for the next hour. After everyone had moved out of the club and dispersed to their cars, I closed up and made my way to my car alone. Domino promised me that he would meet me at home, and at that point I didn't really care if he came home or not. On my way home a call came through from Marlo. I was a little hesitant to answer it, but I picked it up because of the fact that I was still angry at Domino.

"What's up, stranger? I heard you had a big party tonight. How did everything go?"

"Not the way that I planned," I said blandly.

"Well, I'm sorry to hear that. But I was calling you because I wanted to know if it was possible that we could get together to sit down and talk."

"Talk about what?"

"It's some things that I need to talk to you about, and I'd rather do it face to face."

"Well, you can come down to the club early tomorrow and we can talk then."

"That's perfect. I'll see you then, and keep your head up, all right? No nigga should be able to take that away from you."

"All right," I replied, wondering what he meant by that

and how he could have figured that the way that I was feeling right now had anything to do with my man. I made it
home in record time, and after taking a shower I climbed
into bed. When I woke up around 11:00, Domino still hadn't
returned home. I called Marlo and left a message, telling
him that I would be at the club around two. Next I called
Domino on his cell and was surprised that he answered it
on the second ring.

"Hello!"

"I thought that you were coming home last night?" I
asked, annoyed.

"I got caught up."

"Well, it would have been nice to call and tell me that."

"Don't forget I'm a grown-ass man. I don't have to call
and tell you shit!"

"What's your problem, Domino?"

"I don't appreciate the way you showed out last night.
That was some real childish shit."

"Well I didn't appreciate that bitch all up in your face,
but that didn't stop you from talking to her! How dare you
disrespect me like that in my fucking club?" I yelled.

"I'm not going to argue with you, Sugar. I have better
shit to do!"

"What?"

Click.

I stood there looking at the phone for a second since I
couldn't believe that he hung up on me. I wasn't even
going to play myself and call him back. Instead I got
dressed with a "Fuck Him" attitude and was on my way to
the club to meet Marlo. Once I arrived in the parking lot I
noticed Marlo sitting in his car waiting for me. I walked
over and tapped the window.

Looking up, he smiled and opened the driver side
door. "Hey Sugar, I see you're looking delicious as usual."

"Thanks. I didn't expect you to get here so early. It's only 1:30."

"Yeah I bet, but I was really anxious to see you, so I came down and waited. I knew you would be here before two anyway."

"Well let's go in," I said, walking in the direction of the club entrance. I could feel his eyes watching me as he followed my footsteps. "So what's so urgent that you needed to talk to me about?" I said before flicking on the lights.

"It's about Mya."

"I'm not even trying to talk about her. If that all you have to talk about you might as well turn right on back around."

"I feel bad about the way that I did you. I know that you probably won't believe me when I tell you this, but I'm through with her. I've never met a more conniving person in my life, and that isn't something that I can deal with. I believed her lies, but I've been finding out more and more each day."

"More about what?"

"That baby that she was pregnant with isn't mine."

"How do you know that?"

"Because I was hearing a lot of shit, and as soon as the baby was home from the hospital, I had a blood test done."

"Well if it ain't yours then whose is it?" I asked, confused.

"It's by that nigga JT you used to fuck with!"

"What? She doesn't even know JT."

"That's what they wanted you to think. She's trying to hurt you, and I don't know exactly how yet, but I know that she's planning something."

"Where did you hear whatever it is that you think you heard?" I asked anxiously.

"That's not important. I love you, Sugar, and even though I screwed up, I still want another chance to make things right."

"You know that I am with Domino now."

"Yeah, and I also know that you're not happy."

"Look, Marlo, I appreciate the information that you've given me, but right now I can't get into that with you."

"Well I understand, but I need you to know that when you are ready to give us another try, give me a call."

"I'll keep that in mind," I said before standing up to see him to the door.

After he hugged me, I smiled before waving goodbye. I closed the door and instantly began thinking about Mya. I wondered was it really true that she was dealing with JT. How the hell did she know him in the first place, and why would she lie to Marlo about the baby? If it were true, I guess that's how JT knew about Marlo and Mya still sleeping together, but why wouldn't he come clean about the baby if he knew he was the father? I couldn't figure out what was going on, and each time I tried, I came to another dead end.

I left the club puzzled, and it was written all over my face. I decided not to confront either of them with what I was told. I decided to wait around until they approached me. If what Marlo said was at all true, I was sure that it wouldn't be long before it all came to the surface.

Chapter 14

Second Time for Love

After meeting with Marlo I had to get my head back on straight. For the few months that I had been with Domino exclusively, I hadn't laid eyes on Marlo. It was done purposely because I still felt the same way about him, and keeping my distance was the only way to be monogamous with Domino. In a way I was glad to hear that Marlo's relationship with Mya had come to an end, but him not running back to her would be the test. I believed that he still loved me the way that he described, but I wasn't quite ready to let Domino go. Though his behavior had been shady since the night of the party, I had no concrete evidence that he was cheating. In my heart I felt that he was because I knew the signs from all of the previous relationships I had. I also remembered the comment that he made before we were together about expecting a man to cheat. Though I dealt with it before with JT, I refused to settle for that with Domino. I didn't have to, I now knew that I deserved better.

After doing some shopping to gather up some new outfits, I went home to decide on what to wear to the club. It was Friday and the club would be packed. I didn't bother calling Domino because he would have probably given me the cold shoulder anyway. It had been three weeks since the party, and things had been pretty much the same between him and me. We barely saw each other, and when we did it was in passing. I no longer felt like I was in a relationship, and instead of straying away like I usually did, I decided to put an end to it before things really got out of hand. I hesitated a little before calling Marlo. I wanted to get my things out of the house, and I knew that it was virtually impossible for me to do it alone quickly. After three failed attempts to reach him, I gave up.

After going through my routine of getting dressed, I was on my way to open the club. After the first hour the men were packed like sardines from front to back. I put on a happy face as I greeted everyone, trying desperately to hide the fact that I was disgusted over the way that my relationship with Domino had turned out. I hated the fact that after four serious relationships I still hadn't been successful in any of them. I questioned my own behaviors and wondered if I was the cause or if it was just a case of bad luck. Either way I wasn't happy with the way that my life was turning out. The only good thing that I had going for me was the club. I was lucky that Marlo hadn't taken it from me, though things went sour with our relationship he gave me the money for it and promised me that he would never take it away. From the outside looking in, it would appear that my life was turning out exactly how my mother predicted.

On my way to the VIP room I noticed Domino in the back. I hadn't seen him come in, and he was obviously trying to avoid me. Him and a few guys were receiving lap dances, and I was infuriated at Isha, who was pushing every exposed part of her body as close to him as she could get it. I marched over to the booth where Domino was sitting and as soon as Isha noticed my evil stare, she began to move away from him.

"Don't stop dancing. I paid you a lot of money for this!" Domino instructed, grabbing Isha by the arm.

"Yeah, you might as well finish since he's the last customer you'll have in here!" I yelled. "Why are you disrespecting me, Domino?" I asked angrily.

"Look, I'm trying to enjoy myself, and you're ruining it for me!"

"By having this bitch all over you in my club? That's real disrespectful, Dom!" I yelled in frustration.

"What's messed up about it? I'm moving on, and I thought you would have gotten the point by now!"

"This is not the place for this conversation."

"Look, you approached me. I'm through with you, Sugar!" he yelled before standing up.

"Good!" I yelled, before walking toward the door. "And take that bitch with you too, because she's fired!" I was angry but relieved at the same time. I walked to my office and slammed the door and a few minutes later I looked down through the window and noticed Domino leaving the club. I called Marlo on his cell one last time, and he answered on the second ring.

"Hello!" he yelled, over a loud background.

"Hey, I called you earlier. Did you get any of my messages?"

"Yeah, I did."

"Why didn't you call me back?"

"Because, I knew I would be coming out to the club tonight. Where are you anyway? I've been looking for you."

"I'm upstairs in the office, come on up," I said, excited.

"All right."

Once Marlo entered the office and closed the door behind him, he noticed how close I was standing to him.

"Look before you say anything, I want you to know that I really, really miss you."

He smiled, as I moved a little closer and placed my hands on his crotch. I could feel his manhood stiffen and I began to kiss on his neck. I began to move closer, forcing him to back against the door. Once his back was flush with the cherry wood, I unbuttoned his pants and pulled his swollen member through his boxers and quickly met the head with my wet tongue. The taste of the pre-cum caused me to become moist below as I began to massage my clit with my free hand. I could see the delight on his face as I continued to wrap my lips around his length. Each time I could feel the throbbing of his pole begin, I would pull back to prolong the experience. After he could no longer stand the pleasure that I was giving him, he exploded and I consumed every drop. I wanted him inside of me, and before I knew it, he was back at attention and digging deep inside of me on the plush carpet of my office floor. As he pushed my legs in the air as far as they could go, my body began to shiver from the multiple orgasms he was giving me.

"I missed you, baby," he whispered in my ear as he exploded for the second time. He lay on top of me, trying to regain his energy as I enjoyed the scent of his cologne mixed with the aroma of the sex in the air. I was unsure of what to say because I knew he would question my motives for seducing him in the manner that I just had. My only motive was to be happy, and after so much heartache I truly believed that Marlo was the only one that could make me happy. I remembered believing that about every person I had been in a relationship with, but when times were hard for me, Marlo was the one by my side, and for that I was grateful.

After cleaning himself up in the office bathroom, he returned with a smile on his face.

"Why are you smiling?"

"I'm happy. Why is smiling a problem?"

"No, I just wanted to know why, that's all."

"So where do we go from here? I know that nigga ain't treating you right, so are you going to let him go or what?"

"Actually I already have."

"So what does that mean for us?"

"It means that I'm going to give us a second chance."

"I'm real happy to hear that. Are you going to move back in with me?" he said, excited.

"For sure," I said before kissing him. I thought about just getting my own place and finally being independent, but I had been so used to being with someone that I really didn't know how to manage without that comfort of someone to go home to.

I returned to Domino's house the following day to gather up my clothes and take them to Marlo's. I felt a sense of relief as I packed the bags into the back of Marlo's truck. I should have known that Domino meant me no good from day one, but I was blinded, and since I was pissed at Marlo, I didn't see all the signs. I was happy that Marlo and I had found each other again, and it was strange that I didn't know how much I missed him until our lips met. It sent a chill through my body that let me know that with him was where I was supposed to be.

After removing all of my things from Domino's house, I wasn't surprised that he called. I was on my way to the hair salon when my cell phone rang.

"Hello!" I yelled, into the phone.

"I see you went back to that nigga, huh? You don't waist

no time jumping from one bed to the next!" He began laughing, hysterically.

"I guess not, Domino."

"Well, I just wanted to say good luck, for real. I'm sorry about the way things turned out with us, but it was fun while it lasted, and if you ever need anything holla at me."

"Why the kindness now?"

"I don't need any more enemies. I have genuine feelings for you, and I want us to at least be able to remain friends."

"Well friends don't play each other out. If you didn't want to be with me anymore that was all you had to say."

"It ain't that easy for me when I got feelings for someone. I know that I ain't going to change. I'm not ready to settle down with anyone. I'm still enjoying life, and I'd rather you walk out on me than the opposite way around because I would never be able to let you go. Then you would have just been dragging along, and that's not cool."

"I suppose you are right, and I respect you for being honest, but I have some business I need to attend to. I'll be seeing you around."

I didn't plan on being his friend in any way, shape, or form. He had embarrassed me one too many times, and his sorry-ass excuse wasn't nearly enough to mend my wounds. And, yes I may have been a fool for going back to Marlo, but I believed in us.

I entered the salon with a smile on my face. Word traveled fast, and I was sure that Shay had made it her business to tell everyone that Domino and I were through. I was going to make sure each person that thought that I was hurt by the break-up would know I was doing just fine and Marlo was part of the reason for it. All eyes were on me as I switched through the salon to the back where Tammi's chair was.

"What the hell are you so happy about? Didn't you and that nigga Domino break up?" Tammi asked.

"Yup, and I got my man back!"

"Who?"

"Marlo, girl. I moved back in with him and everything, girl. I am so happy."

"Well, I'm happy for you, this time you need to marry that nigga!" she said, laughing.

"Hopefully I will because I'm definitely not letting him go again. You better believe that shit!" I began laughing.

I wanted every chick in there to know that I was where I wanted to be and I was far from being depressed. After leaving the salon I headed home to wait for Marlo. We had agreed to meet there around 4:00 for an afternoon quickie. I showered and waited downstairs on the sofa naked. I was excited when I heard his car pull up in the driveway. Once he entered the house and noticed me sitting there his face displayed the same excitement that I was feeling. He began to take off his clothes as I sat there with my legs spread open, massaging my wetness. He got on all fours and crawled over to the sofa and began to lick me down below. The slow motions of his tongue combined with the thickness of his lips caused me to have an orgasm within seconds.

"I need you inside of me, baby. I need you now!" I moaned, before he lay down on the floor and pulled me down on top of him. After positioning myself with him deep inside of me, I began to make circles with my hips. He began to call my name as I picked up speed and grinded a little harder. I anticipated his explosion, and within ten minutes of me climbing on top of him it happened. I lay on top of him giving him a few soft kisses and whispering how much I loved him in his ear. I was finally leaving all of the bad memories behind. I was finally going to move on and for once be happy with myself. I knew that time would tell, but I was giving him the chance to prove his love for me once and for all. I knew that Marlo stood behind me in anything that I did, and though my business was successful, I still wanted to go to college. For now I would bask in this happiness and spend as much time as I could with him to get back everything that we had before things went downhill. This second chance at love needed to be the last time around for us, and if things went as I had planned it would be.

Chapter 15

Words Will Never Hurt Me . . .

Things between Marlo and I had been picture perfect. If I didn't know any better, I would have sworn it was a dream. The club was still booming, and I had hired someone to run it since I wanted to have more quality time with Marlo. Sugar Walls was the talk of the town—even women would drop by occasionally to see what all of the hype was about.

You know the saying too good to be true? Well, I knew that with my track record a happily ever after was definitely not in the plans. I began receiving weird phone calls, someone breathing then someone laughing. One call was the sounds of someone having sex. I didn't think much of it when they started, but after about a month I begin to grow a little tired of them. Of course the first thing that came to mind was that Marlo was fooling around on me, but he promised me that he hadn't and he was just as clueless as me as to who it was.

The calls would usually come at night, and once I got my number changed, they still managed to get the new one. Letters began pouring in as well. They would always say the same thing, which was basically that I needed to watch my back because they were coming for me. I was afraid, and with the beating I received from Meeka, I knew the pain that could be inflicted if someone was trying to hurt me. I knew that it couldn't have anything to do with Meeka since I had left Dyna alone a long time ago. I knew that it couldn't be Shay because Domino and I were through. The only other person I came up with was Mya, but we were blood, and it was had for me to believe that she would physically hurt me.

Marlo assured me that I had nothing to worry about, and he even bought me a gun to have for protection. I didn't carry the gun around much because I was afraid that if someone did try to attack me I would end up hurting myself with it instead of them. The phone calls and letters soon turned into broken windows and flat tires, and I became even more afraid. Marlo had one of his workers escort me to the club at night and anywhere else that I didn't feel comfortable going.

Once I had a constant bodyguard, the threats began to slow down, and it took a load off of me. I now felt a little less afraid to go outside. On my time away from Marlo, I began to hang out with Marissa a lot. Marissa was in her senior year of college where nursing was her major. She was smart and used the money from the club to further her education, unlike me who had all of my funds collecting dust. I must admit that I was a little jealous of the way things worked out for her, but then I reminded myself that I now had enough money to go to school. With some of my free time I decided that I could sign up for a class or two. Compared to Marissa, we were both smart and we had both shared the same dreams, but mine had gotten so distorted along the way.

On a shopping outing I filled Marissa in on what had been going on with me.

"So you know the threats have slowed down now?"

"What happened?"

"I guess once they noticed the bodyguard they knew it would be hard to get close to me."

"You know that's some real creepy shit. I wouldn't know what to do if I had someone terrorizing me."

"I was scared at first, but after a while I got so used to it that it didn't even bother me much anymore."

"So you still don't have any idea who it is?"

"Nope, but Marlo swears that it's Mya."

"Mya! Why the hell would she do that? You are still her sister even if y'all don't get along."

"I don't know. I don't think it's her, but I don't know who else would dislike me that much."

"Well whoever it is, they definitely have a problem. Hopefully they'll leave you alone soon so you don't have to be looking over your shoulder all the time."

"Yeah, I know."

"Well, how's things with you and Marlo?"

"Good, girl. Things are even better than before. Since I'm not at the club as much we have more time for each other."

After eating lunch I dropped Marissa off and was on my way home when a car bumped me from behind. I thought it was an accident until I looked in the rearview mirror and noticed that the driver wasn't getting out of the car. I loosened my seat belt and was about to get out when the driver began backing up. Soon they rammed the back of my car again, causing me to hit my head on the steering wheel. My vision was a little blurry from the hit, so I couldn't really see who it was in the car. I could tell that it was a woman, and from my past experience I didn't want to wait around for someone to jump out and hurt me. I sped off to get away, and as I continued to look in the rearview mirror I noticed that they were no longer following me. My heart was pounding and my hands were shaking as I tried to keep it together enough to make it home. I called Marlo on his cell as I pulled up in the driveway. Tears begin to flow as soon as I heard his voice.

"What's wrong, baby?" he asked.

"Someone just hit my car!"

"OK, well why are you crying if it was just an accident?"

"It wasn't an accident! They rammed my car again when they noticed me about to get out of the car."

"What? Where was this?" he yelled with concern.

"I was on my way home after dropping Marissa off." I continued to cry.

"Where are you now?"

"Sitting in the car in front of the house. Baby, I'm so scared I'm shaking right now."

"Go in the house and I'll be there in ten minutes, OK? Lock up all the doors."

"OK, please hurry up."

"I will, just go in the house."

I hung up the phone and went into the house like he had instructed. My head was hurting from the hit on the steering wheel. I sat in the living room crying until Marlo came in. Instead of talking he held me in his arms until I broke the silence.

"Why is this happening to me?" I cried.

"I don't know, baby, but I do know that when I find out who'd doing this they are going to pay."

"Do you still think it's Mya?"

"I know that she has something to do with it, and if it is her, she's not going to get away with it."

"I just want to lay down. My head is killing me. Do you think we should call the police?"

"No, I'll handle it. Just go head upstairs. I'm not leaving, I promise."

"OK," I said before heading upstairs to the bedroom.

This event was enough to bring back all of the old memories that I had tried my best to put behind me. I thought that things had settled, but I was wrong. Whoever it was, was not going to give up until they hurt me. In my mind I wished that they would just get it over with already, but in my heart I wanted them to just leave me alone. After I had taken a nap I felt a little better, especially after noticing Marlo by my side. I remembered that I'd left my purse in the car since I had rushed out of earlier. I went downstairs to go out and get it. My balance was a little unsteady since my head was still hurting from the bump.

Once outside I walked to the car and the night was so cold. I felt that there was something wrong, and before I had chance to figure out what it was, it was over . . .

Chapter 16

Marlo: Lost and Found

I woke up to the sound of a tire screeching. I looked to my left and noticed that Sugar had gotten out of bed. I called her name a few times before getting up. I went into the bathroom and when I called her name again, no response. Where the hell was she? I went downstairs and continued to call her name, but still no response. I began to worry, and once I opened the front door and saw her car still parked I was more nervous than I had ever been. I walked up to the car, and before opening the door I saw the strap of a pocket book. I bent down to pick it up and ran into the house to call my boy Rock.

"Yo, Rock, they took Sugar!" I yelled.

"Who took her?"

"I don't know, whoever's been fucking with her! I can't believe this shit, man. How the fuck did they take her from right under my nose, man?" I yelled, before sitting down on the sofa.

"What am I going to do, man? If something happens to her, I'm going to go crazy!"

"I'll be over, man. We'll find her. Don't even stress, all right?"

"I'm getting dressed now. Bring the guns too, man!"

Click.

I got dressed and paced the floor, waiting for Rock to get there. Each minute was another minute that I could have been looking for her, and I was becoming more furious each second. I dialed Mya's number since she was at the top of my list of suspects. She answered the phone on the third ring.

"What's up, baby daddy?" she said with a giggle.

"This ain't no social call, where the fuck is Sugar?"

"You need to keep a leash on her and you won't have that problem anymore."

"I know you are behind this shit, Mya!"

"I don't know what you're talking about, Marlo. I don't know where Sugar is."

"If I find out different, that's your ass! Believe that!"

Click.

Rock was entering the house, and I was ready to explode by that point.

"Did you hear anything yet?" he asked.

"No not yet, let's go find that nigga JT. Because I'm thinking he might have something to do with it too."

"Let's go."

After driving around we were unsuccessful in our efforts to find JT. I went to every spot that I could think of. I even paid a few crackheads with cocaine to find out where he lived. Once we arrived at the house I damn near kicked the door in when no one answered. My mind was racing because I didn't know what to do. I sat down on the step to get my thoughts together when my cell phone rang.

"Hello!" I screamed, into the receiver.

"Looking for me, nigga?"

"Who the fuck is this?"

"The nigga you been looking for. I guess you want to know where your girl is at, huh?"

"I will fucking kill you if you hurt her!"

"You're not in any position to throw out threats."

"Where is she, man?"

"It's not going to be that easy, man. You need to do some things first!"

"I don't have time for games, man. What do you want?"

"$500,000 cash all hundreds in 48 hours."

"That's not enough time to get that together. What the fuck are you trying to pull?" I said, hoping that I could get her back without the money. I didn't know a whole lot about JT, but I've never heard of him being one to be afraid of.

"Well it better be, or she's dead!"

Click.

"Who was that, man?" Rock asked.

"That muthafucker JT. He wants $500,000 in two days or Sugar's dead."

"That nigga is as good as gone!" Rock yelled.

"I can't believe this shit!"

I knew that I needed to get the money to get to Sugar and that nigga JT was dead once I caught up to him. Since I didn't know much about him, I didn't know what to expect. I went back to the house to get the money out of the safe. I bagged up the money in a suitcase and waited around for the next call, which came about three hours later.

"Are you working on the money?" JT asked.

"I got the money, man."

"That was quick. I guess you mean business."

"Yeah, I do."

"Good, because I do too! Bring the money to Dymes Escorts and give it to Dyna. Once she counts it and calls me with the OK, I'll let you know where to find Sugar."

"Dyna! That bitch is in on this too?"

"Just take her the money!"

Click.

The more that was revealed about this the more crazy it sounded. If JT and Dyna were involved, then Mya was definitely a part of it as well. I planned to bury each one of them when it was all over with. Rock and me headed to Dyna's store to make the drop. Dyna unlocked the door and smiled.

"I don't what the fuck you're smiling at!" I yelled.

"Well, hello to you too, Marlo."

"Let's get this shit over with so I can find out where Sugar is."

"No problem. I guess you really love her, huh? I loved her once. I loved the way she made love to me too."

"I'm not trying to hear that shit, Dyna. What the hell do you need money for anyway?" I asked, trying to hold my composure. I was ready to kill this bitch, but I knew that if I did I would probably never find out where Sugar was.

"It's not about money, Marlo. You haven't figured that out? Your girl fucks a lot of people over, especially her sister. She stole you right from under Mya's feet and rubbed that shit all in her face."

"She didn't steal me. I wasn't even dealing with Mya when I got with Sugar."

"That may be true, but you never fuck with your sister's ex either."

"What about you? What did she ever do to you?"

"I gave her the world, I got her away from her crack-head mother, and gave her a new life. She would have never been shit without me, and what did she do? Give me her ass to kiss! I don't take rejection that easily, and she owed me!"

"Why did she owe you anything? She worked for what she had."

"Bullshit! She didn't work nearly enough to get what I gave her."

"And JT? What did she do to him?"

"Embarrassed him."

"Embarrassed him?"

"She made him look like a nut by fucking that nigga Dollar. He hated that shit. Dudes still clown him to this day for that shit."

"He set her up, so how can he be mad at her?"

"That's not the point, Marlo."

"Well, what is the point?"

"Look, she's a bitch and she deserves everything she gets!"

It took everything in me not to strangle her, but I knew that I would never find Sugar if I did. Dyna continued to put the stacks of hundreds into the counter while I sat there burning up inside. It was hard for me to believe that the three of them would do this for the reasons that she described. Their motivation was puzzling me, but I was motivated by pure anger, and when it was all said and done they would be sorry for what they did. After the money was counted she told us to wait outside in the car while she made the phone call to JT.

"Wait outside? Are you fucking crazy? I don't even know if she's alive. Call that nigga JT and tell him to let me hear her voice or something," I yelled. I wasn't about to drop that kind of money and just walk out of here.

"OK, hold on!" she replied. She dialed his number on her cell as I stood there staring her down, watching her every move. "He wants to hear her voice . . . Well what am I supposed to do? He won't leave until he hears her voice . . . Just put her on the phone, JT! . . . Hold on," she said before passing me the phone.

"Hello," I spoke, into the receiver.

"Help me!" she replied, her voice was weak, and I could tell that they had hurt her. I held it together.

"I'm going to get you . . . JT, put her back on the phone!"

"Fuck you, you go outside and wait like she said. I make the fucking rules, nigga!"

I had never been able to take that kind of talk, and once I found her, he was guaranteed to go down. He would soon find out that I meant business and he would see the wrath of a real street nigga. We went outside, she locked the door behind us, and we walked to the car and waited. A few minutes later my phone rang.

"Hello."

"She's out at Fairmount Park."

"Which part? That's a big park!"

"You'll find her!"

Click.

"Let's go, she's in the park somewhere."

We were at the park in a matter of minutes or so it seemed. I drove around for what seemed like hours. It was dark with dim street lighting. The snow that covered the ground made it hard to see. A few times I thought I saw something but was pissed when it wasn't her. After driving around the park a few more times Rock pointed out an area clear of snow. I got out of the car and ran over to what appeared to be a blanket as I got closer. I lifted the blanket and found Sugar frozen underneath.

"Shit! Rock come help me!" I yelled. "Baby, wake up!" I tapped her to try and wake up unsuccessfully.

"Damn, man, get her in the car!"

"I can't believe this, man. What did they do to you?"

I began to cry.

I didn't care that Rock was witnessing my tears. I was about to lose the woman I loved. We jumped in the car and drove to the hospital where the emergency room team worked on her immediately. She had been beaten and her body temperature was so low that it wouldn't register on the thermometer. I was told to sit out in the family waiting area until they could give me more information.

I paced the floor while I waited, and Rock had already left to meet up with my workers to handle JT and Dyna. I would take care of Mya on my own. It felt like hours had passed before the doctor came out to talk to me, and I wasn't prepared for what he was about to tell me.

There were a list of injuries including broken ribs and a broken arm. She had hypothermia from being left out in the snow naked. She was in a coma and not responsive, and the last thing he told me was that she was approximately two months pregnant. It would be at least another hour before I would be able to see her. I buried my face in my hands and began to cry. I should have been there to protect her, and I was in arm's reach. Now she could die and I would never be able to forgive myself if she did.

As soon as I was able to see her I rushed to the room. I could barely recognize her with all of the bumps and bruises. I walked over to the side of the bed and held her hand. I told her how sorry I was and how much I loved her. I would stay by her side and I hoped that she could feel my presence.

Chapter 17

Sugar: Beginning of Life

I opened my eyes unsure of where I was, but I soon realized that I was in a hospital. I noticed Marlo over in a chair asleep. I wasn't in any pain, but I didn't know why I was there. I began to call Marlo's name, which was in a low tone as I struggled to raise my voice. Soon he woke up and looked around the room.

"It's me, baby," I spoke as loud as I could.

"Baby, you're awake!" he said, running over to the bed.

"What happened to me?"

"Let's not talk about that right now. You're OK now, that's all that matters," he said, kissing my forehead. "Let me get the doctor OK?" He went to the door and called for a doctor.

I lay in the bed crying. I couldn't remember what happened to me that landed me here in the hospital.

A few doctors and nurses ran into the room and began looking me over and asking me a list of random questions like my name, what year it was, and if I knew where I was. I was still unsure of what happened to me, but I knew it must have been bad because I obviously had been out of it for a while. It was hard to me to talk because I didn't have a lot of energy. I was drained. I felt stiff and it was hard for me to move around. After everyone left the room, I began to question Marlo again.

"Baby, what happened? Why am I here?"

"Somebody tried to take you away from me, baby."

"Who?" I asked, as I continued to cry.

"I don't want to upset you by telling you that. Let's wait until you get a little better."

"I need to know, Marlo. How long was I asleep?"

"Three weeks!"

"Three weeks? What the hell happened?"

"I found you outside in the snow, and you had been beaten really bad."

"Do you know who did it to me?" I asked, confused.

"I do but I don't want to tell you now. How about some good news?"

"What good could have possibly came out of this?"

"You're pregnant, baby!" he smiled.

"Pregnant? Are you serious? How far along? How do you know that?"

"Almost three months now. The doctors told me. That's good, right?"

"That is good, baby. I can't believe that," I said, rubbing my hands over my stomach.

"Well, it's true."

"So how's the club, is everything OK?"

"The club is fine. They're holding it down for you. Tina has been great helping Tracey learn the ropes of running the club. I can't wait to call them so they can set up your welcome home party. They've been waiting to hear from me."

"I'm glad to hear that."

Marlo and I talked for hours before I drifted off to sleep. I woke up a few times as flashbacks of being beaten popped in my head. I could hear a familiar voice over and over again, but I couldn't put my finger on who it was. Marlo still hadn't told me who attacked me, but I knew that with the flashbacks I would soon figure it out.

I stayed in the hospital for another week before I was released. The ride home was a long one, and I though I was happy to get out of the hospital, I was really nervous since I still didn't know exactly what happened to me. I hated the fact that I was going home blind to what happened. I was quiet the entire ride home; I couldn't think of anything that I wanted to say to Marlo since he was still being so secretive about what happened. Once we pulled up into the driveway Marlo turned off the car and looked at me as if he had some bad news to spill.

"What's wrong?" I asked.

"I'm just glad that you're coming home. I didn't think that you were going to make it. Before we go in, I just wanted to tell you that my little man is here. He's going to be staying with us."

"Why? Where is Mya?"

"I am going to get custody of him so that I can guarantee that he's well taken care of."

"But I don't understand. Where is she? And who's watching the baby? She's not going to fight you on that?"

"She can't fight me, and my mom is watching the baby," he replied.

"Why not?"

"Because she's in jail."

"Jail? For what?" I asked, stunned.

"We'll talk about it later, but let's go in and get you settled for now."

"Why do you keep doing that, Marlo? I'm not made of glass, I won't break! I need you to stop beating around the bush and be honest with me. What the hell is going on?" I yelled in frustration. I wanted to know the truth. I was tired of being shielded like a child.

"I'm sorry if I'm trying too hard to take care of you, but I almost lost you and I just don't want to upset you."

"I need the truth, that's all I'm asking for."

"JT, Dyna, and Mya were all a part of what happened to you."

"What?" I asked, confused.

"Mya went to Dyna to come up with a strategy to get revenge on you. Dyna hooked her up with JT and that's when they started messing around. That was around the time that he approached you telling you that I was still dealing with Mya. JT got her pregnant to then blame it on me and when we broke up, she was happy and I was in a relationship with her until I found out about the baby. Once I left, she was furious. She threatened to never let me see my son, and once I got back with you, the phone calls and stuff started."

"Yeah, I remember that," I said.

"Once you went missing, that nigga JT called me asking for $500,000 in cash to get you back. I had to drop the money off to Dyna, and once it was counted, JT called me and told me I could find you out in the park. I searched for you for hours, and when I found you, you were tied up, naked, and unconscious."

"What? I can't believe that. Tell me that's not true," I cried. "Marlo, tell me that's not true!" I screamed.

"I'm sorry, baby, that's why I didn't want to tell you."

"Why would they do that to me?"

"Dyna gave me a bullshit explanation for all of it."

"And what was that?"

"She said you stole me from Mya, you gave her your ass to kiss, and you embarrassed JT."

"They did this to me for that?"

"That's what she said."

"Well I hope all of them rot in jail!"

"Well, Mya will, but the other two will rot in hell!"

"What do you mean by that?"

"They aren't with us anymore. I made sure of that."

"You killed them?"

"No, not with my own hands," he replied.

"What did you do, Marlo? I can't have you in jail too!" I cried.

"It will never come back to me, baby. I promise."

"I knew that Mya hated me, but I would have never thought she would do this to me."

"I know it's a lot to grasp, but you'll be OK. They are out of our lives for good."

"Give me a minute to get myself together. I'll be in the house in a few minutes."

"I don't want to leave you out here alone."

"It's OK. I'll be fine."

"Don't be too long."

"I won't," I replied.

I sat in the car crying hysterically for a few minutes. I was beyond hurt by what Marlo had just told me. I never hurt anyone that much to warrant being kidnapped and left for dead. How could my own sister be involved in something so sinister? I could remember growing up and Mya wanting to be exactly like me. She would follow me everywhere and would emulate my every move. It wasn't until the teenage years that we began to grow apart. After our fall out I missed her because we had begun to mend the relationship. I never wanted to take her man away. It was never in my plans, but the conniving ways of Dyna only made it inevitable to stay away. I did regret many of the decisions I made in my life, but being with Marlo wasn't one of them. After I cried as much as I could, I wiped my face and got out of the car. Marlo was standing in the door waiting for me.

"Are you OK?" he asked, reaching his arms out.

"Yeah, I'm OK," I said before hugging him.

For the next few weeks I stayed in most of the time, but I knew that I had to get out sooner or later. I was used to being out and about, and that house thing was going to grow old quick. Though I knew the people who hurt me were out of the picture I still was a little afraid to go out in the street. In my heart I felt that it was still something lurking, but I didn't know exactly what it was. Staying in was keeping me in a down mood, and getting a breath of fresh air may have been just what I needed. Babysitting my nephew most of the time constantly reminded me of my sister, and I decided to go visit her at the prison. I needed to see her face to face and find out why she hurt me the way that she did. Marlo was totally against it, but I explained that it was the only way for me to move on.

On visiting day the following week I drove up to the correctional facility where she was being held until she went to trial. I was nervous as they led me to the visitors waiting area. I was surprised that she accepted my visit but I was glad that she did. My stomach was in knots as she came to the table where I was sitting. I didn't know where to begin as she sat down in front of me with a blank stare. Her hair was pulled back into two braids and she looked much thinner than she had the last time I'd seen her. Each time I tried to make eye contact, she would look away avoiding my stare. I assumed that she may have been embarrassed for me to see her in that state.

"So, I'm sure you're surprised to see me here?" I spoke in a low tone.

Silence . . .

"Why did you accept my visit if you didn't want to talk to me?" I asked.

"I don't know what to say," she replied.

"You could start by telling me why you did what you did to me."

"I don't know, I guess I let my anger get the best of me."

"So what was it supposed to solve by having me killed, and what was the point of asking for the money?"

"I didn't want the money, but we had to pay JT to kidnap you. He wanted more money than we wanted to give him, so the ransom was the only way for him to get it. I didn't even know that he asked for money until Dyna told me."

"You expect me to believe that?"

She changed her tone. "It's the truth!"

"So is that supposed to make everything better because you didn't want the money? You wanted him to kill me, Mya!"

"He was only supposed to scare you, that's all. Dyna and him changed the plan without telling me anything. They didn't do anything that I asked, they did what they wanted to."

"Well since they're both dead now I guess I'll never hear their side of the story."

"Dead?" she asked, confused.

"Oh you didn't know? Well I hate to break the news to you, but they were taken care of. Too bad you felt guilty and confessed, huh? You might have been able to enjoy a little bit of the money you stole from my man!"

Silence . . .

"I just had to come here because I need to move on. I'm

going to take good care of your son. I just want you to
know that. He's my blood and he did nothing wrong, so
don't ever think I would mistreat him because of you. Be-
sides, he's about to have a little brother or sister soon
and—"

"What?" she asked.

"Yeah, I'm pregnant." I rubbed it in because I felt that
she needed to experience some of the pain that I felt.

"Isn't it bad enough that you stole him away from me?
You're going to get pregnant by him and I'm the one
that's fucked up? Now, I don't feel sorry for what happened to you. I wish they would have found you a few minutes later and your ass would have froze to death," she spat
with evil eyes.

"I knew you had it in you, the little sorry act wasn't you.
This is the real Mya—hateful and deceitful."

"Fuck you, Sugar!" she said, rising from her seat.

"Don't screw up and get yourself more time in here!
Then you'll have more time to dream about me and Marlo
living it up!"

"I hate you!" she screamed before jumping over the
table, attempting to grab me. The guards ran over and
handcuffed her before she got a chance to assault me. She
continued to yell obscenities as they removed her from
the visiting area. One of the remaining guards showed me
out of the room after asking me if I was OK.

I was OK, and I felt like a little weight had been lifted
off of my shoulders. I had gotten a chance to see Mya for
who she really was, and no amount of make-up could
cover those dark spots. On the drive home I thought
about my future and the new life that I was bringing into
this world. I rubbed my stomach and smiled. I dialed
Marlo on his cell to let him know that I was OK.

"Hello?"

"Hey, baby, where are you?"

"In the barbershop getting a shape up. How did everything go?"

"Let's just say it turned out the way that I expected."

"Well, how do you feel?"

"I feel great. Where's little man at?"

"At my mom's, why?"

"I need you to meet me at home when you're done. I need you to come hold me and make love to me."

"Are you OK?"

"I'm fine, I just need my man to come home and take care of me. What's wrong with that?"

"Nothing at all. I'll be there."

"Good, I'll be waiting."

Once I made it home I went up to the master bedroom and drew a bath in the Jacuzzi with lavender. I took off each piece of clothing and pulled my hair up into a ponytail before getting into the water. About five minutes after I was in the Jacuzzi relaxed I heard Marlo calling my name.

"I'm in here, baby," I yelled.

He entered the bathroom and smiled as I stood up out of the Jacuzzi displaying my naked body that was dripping wet. I motioned with my hands for him to come closer and he obeyed. I began to kiss him in the most passionate way. I had never been this excited about seeing him before. I wanted to make love to him for hours and show him how much I loved him. I helped him undress and as he stood in front of me I kissed and sucked every inch of his muscular chest. I instructed him to sit on the edge of the tub so that I could take his length into my mouth. He moaned as I wrapped my lips around his pole and flickered my tongue as I cupped his jewels with my free hand. He rubbed his hands on my back as I moved him in and out of my mouth.

When it was too much for him to handle, he moved me to the same position to return the favor. With my legs wide open he began to lick my clit in slow strokes, forcing me to explode. He pushed the thickness of his tongue inside my tunnel, he continued to massage my clit with his fingers. Once he stuck his fingers inside of me and returned to my clit with his tongue, I exploded again and he smiled when he noticed the trance that his tongue and finger action had put me in.

I had never had sex underwater before, and I had never imagined how intense it would be until he was deep inside of me with the Jacuzzi jets pounding against my back. I screamed his name over and over again as he hit my G-spot, causing one orgasm after another. I licked his ear and whispered how much I loved him as he slowed down the strokes and dug deeper inside of me. When he exploded he screamed that he loved me too, and I smiled inside and out. My man loved me!

Chapter 18

Never Loved Any More . . .

The next few months went better than I could have ever expected. Winter was rolling around, and I hoped that the cold weather would only give me and Marlo more time to snuggle up. We were awaiting Mya's trial, and I wanted to get it over and done with. At this point I was a week away from my due date, and I was about ready to explode. My huge belly and swollen feet were far different than how I'd imagined my pregnancy would be. Marlo made it his business to let me know how beautiful I was even at 200 pounds. I had recently decided to put the club up for sale because I wanted to leave that part of my life behind with the list of other things I wanted to get past as well. I had to go down and show the property almost every day to prospective buyers. No one had offered to pay my asking price yet in the two months the for-sale sign had been posted.

Almost every day since my seventh month of pregnancy I went to the spa daily for massages and facials. It was so relaxing and necessary to get me through the long months of pregnancy. I could barely drive, so Marlo world drop me off at the Center City Spa and return to pick me up when I was done. It was Friday and I had dragged myself out of bed, exhausted from running around the day before. Marlo had just pulled off when I began to get shooting pains in my abdomen. I sat down on the bench in the waiting area as I waited for the pain to subside. The receptionist came over and asked if I was OK after noticing my obvious state of pain.

"Are you OK, Ms. Clark?"

"I'm just having contractions, that's all," I said, breathing heavily trying to channel the pain.

"Are you sure you want to go in? Maybe you should go to the hospital."

"I'm OK, I—" Before I could finish the sentence another intense contraction stopped me. "Could you call this number for me, and tell him that he needs to come back and get me?" I asked, passing her my cell phone, which displayed Marlo's cell number.

I sat on the bench waiting for him to arrive as the contractions began to get closer together. By the time Marlo ran into the spa, they were five minutes apart and tears were pouring out of my eyes. He was excited but nervous as he sped down Broad Street to get me to Temple University Hospital. After pulling up to the emergency room I was immediately taken up to Labor and Delivery. I cried as the pain became more intense by the minute.

Once examined by the doctor, I was five centimeters dilated—five away from where I needed to be to start pushing. Marlo was excited and ignored the sarcastic remarks I made due to the pain I was experiencing. The pain medicine that the nurse gave me through the IV was no longer working, and I was growing more uncomfortable.

"I need something else for pain, I can't take this anymore," I yelled as I grabbed hold of the pillow to try and breathe past the pain.

"Baby, you're almost there. You've done so good," Marlo spoke, holding my hand.

I cried for the next hour until they checked me again, and I nearly flipped when they told me I hadn't made any progress. The pain was excruciating, and my entire body was trembling from it. Two hours later I still hadn't progressed any further, and with the baby's continued dips in heart rate, the doctors decided to give me a Cesarean section.

I was nervous as they wheeled me down to the operating room. I kissed Marlo once more before they took me in. Marlo was ushered to the waiting area since I would be put to sleep under the emergency circumstances.

When I woke up in the recovery room, Marlo was sitting by my side with our baby girl in his arms. When I held her, I felt chills go through me because though I loved Marlo with all my heart, this little girl consumed it as soon as I looked at her. I thought about all of the trouble that I had gone through since leaving my mom's, and at this point it was all fading away. You never really know how good it feels to be a mother until you actually experience it yourself. I was in love with them both, and I now believed that a happily ever after was possible after all. **I never knew that I could love anyone more** than Marlo, but that idea was out the window now.

After debating over a name for the baby we came up with Skyy Janae Billups. She had fair skin like mine, but she was the spitting image of her father. She definitely made me fall in love with him all over again. I was in a lot of pain once the pain medication from surgery began to wear off, and once I was comfortable again I sat with my family and enjoyed them.

The four days I stayed in the hospital seemed like an eternity, and I was excited to get home and lay in my own bed. Marlo surprised me by having the nursery set up. I had planned to do it myself before I went into labor, but Skyy had her own plans. I was ready to walk down the road of motherhood and it was going to be much easier once the club was gone. I looked through the list of buyers bidding for the club and ended up selling for $10,000 less that my asking price to the highest bidder. Skyy had given me the boost that I needed to just get rid of it, and I wanted to have more time for her and her brother.

On the first day of Mya's trial I was sick to my stomach. I didn't want to go to court, but I knew I had no other choice. Marlo dropped the kids off at his mom's, and we began the drive to the court house. The court room was packed with people, including the press. It had been a highly publicized case, and though I knew it would be packed, I didn't know to what extreme.

Once Mya was escorted into the court room we never made eye contact. I wasn't ready to testify, but I knew there was no other way to get justice. The prosecutor and defense attorney both made their opening statements to the charges of conspiracy and solicitation to commit murder and third degree assault and assault for hire. The defense tried to use the death of Mya's first born as a temporary insanity plea and stated that she wasn't in any condition to sign a confession, which she did without an attorney present.

I was pissed that she would try to get out of this, and I wasn't going to allow that to happen. The following day when it was my turn to take the stand I had a new attitude and I was ready to bury her under the jail. The courtroom was silent as the prosecutor began to question me.

"Ms. Clark, how do you know the defendant?"

"She's my sister."

"So were you two close? How was your relationship?"

"No, we haven't been close for some time now. Probably since we were little kids."

"So what happened to the close relationship you had?"

"I really don't know. I tried to be her friend, but she always pushed me away."

"So what motivated the alleged attack?"

"Well, she never told me exactly what motivated her."

"But she did admit to it?"

"Yes she did. When I went to visit her in prison she told me that she was behind it and she even tried to attack me when I told her that I was pregnant."

"So she admitted that she planned to have you kidnapped and assaulted?"

"Yes."

The line of questioning went on for nearly an hour, and once the defense began to question me it took just as long. The day was exhausting, and I was glad when it was over.

The day that the jury read the verdict I couldn't believe what I was hearing, so much so that it was like a TV on mute. They found her guilty of all four charges, and she could possibly spend the rest of her life in prison. After leaving the courtroom I was quiet, and I began to think more about the future and the fact that I would have to be a mother to her child forever if she was sentenced to a life term.

Once we were home I sat down and before Marlo left to get the kids, I told him to sit so that we could discuss the things that were on my mind. I had been really stressed lately, and I needed him to understand what was going on with me.

"I need you to stop selling drugs, Marlo."

"What? You know I can't do that."

"You have to, we have two children to think about, and we have enough money to survive."

"Surviving is not enough. I need to maintain what I have now, and a nine to five won't cover it."

"Marlo, I'm serious. I want to go back to school, and I want us to be a family, but I can't keep going to sleep every night wondering if I'll ever see you again."

"I can't, Sugar. This is all I've ever done, and I don't know if I can do anything else."

"I need you to be here for us, and it's not guaranteed if you keep living like this."

"Life isn't guaranteed period! I have to do what I have to do, and I don't want to talk about this anymore," he said before rising from the sofa.

"Marlo, please," I begged.

"I'll talk to you later. I'll be back with the kids by seven," he said before walking out of the house.

I cried because I knew that I couldn't live without him and I didn't want be a single mother. I wanted life for the children to be so much different than that, and I prayed that he would come around before it was too late. It bothered him that I was demanding him to stop, and I understood that he would have to make that decision on his own if it was ever going to happen. I knew that you couldn't force a man to make a decision like that, and all I could do is sit back and pray for the best.

For the next few weeks Marlo and I barely saw each other. I was beginning to think that he was cheating again, and I wasn't ready to deal with that. His quick visits home were thinning out, and I wasn't sure what I needed to do. I missed making love to him and I missed spending quality time. From the day that I demanded he stopped distributing drugs, I was lucky if he even looked me in the eye. I begged him to talk to me and tell me what was going on, but each time he said that he was too busy and had some runs to make.

When it was time for Mya to be sentenced I decided not to go to court. I contacted the prosecutor after it was final and found that Mya would spend the next fifteen years in prison before she would be eligible for parole. Though I felt that she deserved everything that she got, deep down inside I wished that she could walk away from this. I wished that it had never happened, and she and I could be the close friends that we once were. Marlo wasn't around when I got the news, and when I told him he acted as if he didn't really car either way.

I was losing my grip, and each day I was getting closer to snapping. I needed Marlo to be there for me now the way that he had been in the past. I needed him to hold me when I was upset and reassure me that everything was going to be OK. Instead he was out in the streets while I was home with two kids playing mommy.

Chapter 19

The Truth, No More Lies . . .

After I began to give up on Marlo again I started spending time out. I was tempted everyday, and I tried my best to keep out of the life that I lived before. I didn't want to cheat, and even if Marlo had resorted to that, I was going to be the bigger person this time. I stopped begging him to come home, and when he did I ignored his presence. I could tell that it was beginning to piss him off.

I had decided to play chef and cook a nice dinner. I went out to the supermarket and grabbed everything that was on the ingredients list for a new recipe I wanted to try. It was a Teriyaki chicken and rice meal that I thought would be good. I was in the kitchen beginning to set everything up when Marlo came in and picked the baby up out of the bassinet. After noticing me cooking, he came in and looked around.

"What are you doing?" he asked, looking me up and down.

"Well, hello! And I'm cooking what does it look like?"

"Since when did you start cooking?"

"Maybe if you'd come home more often, you would know!" I spat.

"Whatever!" he said.

"Marlo, why don't you just be a man and tell me that you want this to be over? I'm tired of playing games. If it's somebody else that you want to be with you need to speak up!"

"Who said anything about anybody else?

"You haven't touched me in damn-near a month. I'm not dumb. We've been down this road before, and the last time you were screwing someone else." I hoped that my yelling wouldn't scare the baby, but I was pissed and I couldn't lower my tone. I was glad that his son was at his mom's because he would have definitely been upset by us arguing.

"This is not before, and I don't have time to argue with you right now!" he yelled.

"You never have time for anything anymore. You might as well never come back!" I yelled, angrily.

"What?"

"You heard me! I'm tired, Marlo. **I'm asking you for the truth, no more lies!** Do you want to be with me or not?"

"I'm not going to answer that."

"Fuck you, Marlo!" I said, turning my back to him.

"I'm not going to answer it because I . . . Never mind. I'm out of here!" he said before placing the baby back into the bassinet and leaving out.

I continued to cook and I actually felt a little better since telling him how I felt. At this point I wanted him to make a decision one way or the other so I could deal with it the way that I needed to. I knew that Marlo wouldn't come home that night, so I didn't worry when he didn't show up. I did worry when a week went by and I hadn't heard anything from him. Even when he was angry with me for whatever reason he would never go a day let alone a week without popping in to see the kids.

I didn't know how to contact many of his friends. The only one that I knew how to contact was Rock. I dropped the kids off at Marissa's and went out looking for Rock. It was two hours before I found him and he just happened to be driving by when I beeped the horn and got him to pull over. I walked over to the car and immediately noticed the look on his face. He wasn't happy to see me at all.

"What's up, Sugar?"

"Have you seen Marlo?"

"He hasn't called you?" he asked, surprised.

"No, I haven't talked to him all week and I'm scared. Do you know where he is?"

"I do, but if he hasn't called he probably doesn't want you to know where he is."

"Rock, please. I need to know if he's OK."

"Sugar I can't."

"Please!" I begged.

"Look, he's in the hospital."

"What?" I said, as tears began to well up in my eyes.

"See, that's probably why he didn't want to tell you."

"What happened, where is he?" I began to get hysterical.

"Calm down. Look, get in the car."

"Tell me where he is!"

"Get in the car and stop tripping. People starting to stare and shit!"

I walked around to the passenger side and sat down in the seat. Uneasy, I began to speak and he shut me up in seconds.

"Look, he'll be out of the hospital tomorrow. He got shot in the leg the other night down north and . . ."

"He got shot? What?" I began to cry hysterically.

"He's OK. He was only hit in the leg. He didn't want you to know what happened and he's going to kill me for telling you."

"What hospital is he in?"

"I've told you enough already. He'll be home tomorrow."

"I need to go see him."

"Look I have somewhere to go, but I'll see if I can get him to call you."

"Rock, please."

"I'll try and get him to call you. That's the best that I can do."

I finally gave up since I realized that I couldn't get any more information from him. I couldn't believe Marlo would have concealed this type of information from me. I knew that he was angry with me when he left, but I couldn't imagine why he would go without telling me that he'd been shot. I began to get angry as the hours passed after seeing Rock without a phone call from Marlo. I sat in the living room, staring at the wall, and when the phone finally rung I nearly broke my neck trying to run and answer it.

"Hello!"

"Hey, baby."

"Marlo, what the hell happened? Why didn't you call me?"

"Because I didn't want you to go crazy worrying about me."

"I was getting sick worrying. How could you not tell me, Marlo?"

"I'm sorry, baby."

"What's going on that you can't talk to me? What's happening to us?"

"I've just been trying to tie up some loose ends. I'm trying to make things better for us, and then this shit happened. I didn't want you to be worried if I told you the things that I needed to do. There was no other woman, and I never wanted you to think that. I love you and I'm trying to make some changes for our future."

"Like what, Marlo?" I asked, confused.

"We'll talk when I get home."

"Do you promise to come home to me?"

"I promise that I'll be there tomorrow."

"OK, I love you, Marlo."

"I love you too," he said before hanging up.

I loved him more than I thought possible. I had never worried about anyone that much in my entire life, and from that I knew we were meant to be together. I was able to sleep that night knowing that my man was coming home and that we would be able to patch things up.

The following day I woke up excited about seeing Marlo. I cleaned the house and since I figured it would be at least after lunch before he would come home, I went out to the market to buy a few things to cook. As each hour passed I got more anxious, and when I heard his car pull into the driveway I ran out the door to greet him. Even after being released from the hospital just hours before my man looked as good as if he was never shot in the first place. He smiled when he noticed how happy I was to see him. Once I wrapped my arms around him, I never wanted to let go.

"I missed you so much. Please don't ever do that to me again!" I said as a tear of happiness welled up in my eye. I held on tight.

"I won't," he said before kissing me. We walked toward

the house, and after entering I immediately began my line of questioning.

"So what is it that you've been trying to do?" I asked.

"I've been trying to get out of the game like you asked me to. It's not easy to just up and walk away. I had to tie up every loose end, and I still ended up getting shot over some bullshit. I felt bad when it happened because I snapped on you when you asked me to quit. I'm a man and it bothered me that you were trying to tell me what to do. After I got shot I really began to think. I've been shot before, but this time was so much different because of you and the kids. I don't want you to have to deal with me dying when I could have just walked away. I've never felt the way that I feel about you, and I don't want to lose you. I made a decision to leave that shit alone for you, and I'm going to do my best to never go back. I need you to be with me forever, and this is from my heart," he said before bending down on one knee. I nearly drowned myself in tears as they began to flow instantly. I couldn't believe what he was about to do and I was speechless as he removed the huge four-karat princess cut diamond ring from its box.

"Will you marry me?" he asked, gently sliding the ring on my left hand. "Say something, baby!"

"Yes, I'll marry you, yes!" I kissed him.

"You had me scared for a second there."

"I love you so much," I said with a huge smile on my face.

I moved closer to him and kissed him sensuously. He began to rub his hands over my back as I palmed the back of his head to get a deeper kiss. I moaned as he slid his hands into my shorts and began to massage my clit. I pulled my tank top over my head and forced my breast into his mouth. He began to savor the taste of my erect nipple as I pulled his manhood through his pants and slowly stroked it. I wanted him inside of me since it had been weeks since we'd been together. I begged him to make love to me, and he told me to hush while he satisfied me. He carried me upstairs to the bedroom, and after laying me down on the bed he pulled my shorts off and began to feast on my wet mound. The orgasms began to come one after another, and after I could no longer control them I tried to free myself from his grip. He instantly pulled me back and continued to work on me down below.

Soon he stood up and turned me over so that my butt was pointed up. He slowly entered me from behind made slow circles inside of my tunnel. He hit my G-spot and soon I could feel the juices pour out of me. He moaned loudly as the extra lubrication intensified the experience. He turned me over, and my legs rested on his shoulders. He made long, steady strokes, and with each orgasm I screamed his name. Marlo knew how satisfied I was by the puddle that was lying under me. I lost count of the orgasms after the fifth one. I was almost comatose by the time he exploded.

We lay there looking at each other, and I was smiling because things were now heading in the right direction. I placed my head on his chest as thoughts of the future ran through my mind. I was finally going to be with the man I loved. My life had come full circle, and I believed that things could only get better from that point. I was speechless, but he managed to get one sentence out of me before I drifted off to sleep.

"How much do you love me, baby?" he asked, as he ran his fingers through my hair.

I raised my head, gazed into his eyes, and simply said, "More than you could ever imagine!"

Epilogue

I began planning our wedding immediately following the engagement. I planned a huge ceremony in Hawaii. The guest list was a total of 200 people, and I was surprised to see that everyone made it. I found out shortly after the honeymoon that I was pregnant again, and Marlo was overly excited. I gave birth to another little girl that we named Lynise Jade. I fell in love with her as soon as I saw her, just as I had with Skyy.

Sugar Walls was renamed after it was bought, and it was now called Movers and Shakers. I peeped in from time to time just to revisit what was once a huge moneymaker for me. I eventually enrolled in Temple University studying social work and I graduated exactly four years later with a Bachelor's degree. I had finally accomplished what had been my dream for so long, and I wished that my mother had been alive to see how wrong her predictions about me were.

Marlo eventually opened up a barbershop and gave a lot of young barbers a chance to shine in the neighborhood. The shop thrived, and I was glad that he found another hustle—something more productive and less dangerous. I no longer had to worry about him being shot or killed, and that made it a lot easier for me to sleep at night.

I visited Mya frequently with my nephew, and each time she apologized for the things that she had done. I forgave her because it wasn't all her fault. I blamed my parents for the way we were raised, and I blamed myself for part of the way that I had treated her. I wasn't sorry for any of the things that I had done, but I knew that I was partly responsible. Going to church was one of the things that helped me because I had never been to church growing up. I never even thought about it until I turned my life around. I even convinced Marlo to go with me twice a month. Believing in God healed me, and I was able to move on.

I thought about all of my relationships and how they all affected my life, starting with my parents. I never really got a chance to know them. The drugs that clouded their minds only allowed the abuse and blocked any form of closeness. I vowed to treat my children totally opposite of that. My relationships with everyone else molded me, and I believe that they helped me. I always felt like I needed to be with someone to validate myself, and now things were totally different.

I thought about the things that I went through often, and though many of the memories weren't good ones, I know that each experience made me stronger. I could have never survived the things that I had without the bad times to make my spine a little tougher. I finally realized how a *few seconds of pleasure can lead to a lifetime of a pain,* and you should never be so dependent on affection that you lose control of your soul. I realized my mistakes, and Marlo realized his. We finally saw the importance of taking responsibility for our own actions. We both wanted the best for our children, and that was part of the reason I became a social worker. I didn't want anyone to live the life that I did, and any way that I could prevent it early I was going to try. The saying that everything happens for a reason was finally making sense to me, and it meant a lot knowing that my success didn't come easy. I had to work hard for everything that I had, and it made it that much easier to enjoy it.

COMING SOON FROM
Q-BORO
BOOKS

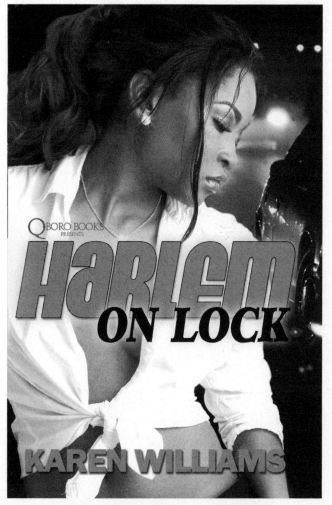

JANUARY 2008
1-933967-34-X

HARLEM ON LOCK

BY KAREN WILLIAMS

Clad in a slinky black dress that stopped at the bottom of my thighs and had an open back that went all the way to my rump and some heels, I stepped out with Chief in a silver Benz. The car drove so smooth I felt like I was floating as he cruised on the highway. He took me to a fancy restaurant called Crustacean. I had never been to a restaurant that fancy. There was even someone playing the piano. It was crazy. We were served lobster and some prawns that looked like huge shrimp. I couldn't get enough, and he ordered lobster tail after lobster tail. I was sopping the meat in so much butter, my fingers were greasy. Chief just laughed and told me to eat as much as I wanted.

He didn't have to tell me twice.

He poured some wine for me. I had never drank the stuff before. But he said I needed it to unwind. So I allowed myself two glasses of the stuff before pushing the pretty glass away. I didn't want to make a habit of having any addictions or weaknesses. I had seen first hand how they can ruin a person's life.

When I was too stuffed to eat any more, he took me home. That sounded so weird to me then, but that's what it was to me now.

Once we arrived, Chief wrapped his arm around my waist and guided me into the master bedroom. His room I guessed. It was in the part of the house I hadn't been invited to see.

It was larger than mine and had a definite man's touch in the way it was decorated. Everything from the carpet to the bed and decorations were coal gray and black, from the big-ass rug that looked and felt like real fur when I rubbed my feet against it, to the blankets on his bed. There was a wide-ass fish tank in the room with all types of weird looking fish swimming around, and a fireplace. Chief must have been obsessed with those flat-screen TV's, because there was another one in his room.

I smiled when I saw rose petals on the floor leading a trail to the bed.

Chief stood behind me and slipped my dress off my shoulders so I was in only my underwear and heels, shivering slightly because I was a little nervous about what was about to happen.

He slipped down on both his knees, pulled off my shoes, and slipped my panties off so I was totally nude. Then he pulled me into the bathroom where there was a huge Jacuzzi tub filled to the top with water and suds.

"Go ahead and get in," he told me.

I did and shyly watched him undress until he was nude like me. He was a big, husky nigga—powerfully built with a muscular chest, arms bigger than my thighs, and muscular legs. He had a hairy body with a trail of silky hair that started at his pecs and led a trail down his stomach to his—Lord—big-ass dick that looked like it belonged on a horse not on a man.

Chief joined me in the tub. Like a baby he bathed me gently, starting from my feet and going up my legs. His hands were having an effect on my body. The shit felt good too. I didn't know if it was OK for it to feel that good, but it did. He then took a shampoo that smelled like coconuts and washed every inch of my hair. His hands rubbed all over my body, and where his hands stopped, his kisses begin.

"Damn, baby, you fine as hell."

He gave me gentle pecks all over my skin. Then he used his tongue. He pulled me into his lap and began kissing me slowly, first a peck, then my bottom lip was in his mouth and he taught me how to use my tongue to play with his. Soon, it became second nature to me. My hands curled around his neck and I was returning his kiss with passion.

He lifted me to my feet. Water splashed as he lifted me out of the tub, carried me into his room and placed me on his bed. I lay on my back totally nude. The way he stared down at me made me feel like I was a feast.

His mouth began working from my neck to my collar bone to the mounds of my breasts. He went lower and kissed my stomach and my hips. Then he raised my thighs and placed kisses on the inside of each. He placed more on my ankles. When he got to my feet, he took each one and nibbled on my toes, making me squeal.

Then he spread my legs apart and put his head between them. I felt his tongue enter me, setting my insides on fire. I cringed and twisted my body every which way from the pleasure. As he licked me like I was an ice cream cone, he used his fingers in pleasurable spots then followed with his tongue. His hand kept flittering on my clit while his tongue eased in and out of me. When my legs started shaking and I felt a weird sensation take over my body, cum oozed out he lapped it up with his tongue.

"Your pussy taste good, baby," he said in a husky voice. Then he settled between my legs and entered me.

There was no pain, just an intense pleasure as my walls were stretched to accommodate his dick.

His eyes bore down in mine and he asked, "You like what Daddy doing to you, Harlem?"

I moaned, losing control.

He kept the tempo extra slow.

He started playing with my breasts, licking them and squeezing my nipples. He guided himself in and out of my pussy smoothly. With my legs gripped tightly around him, a weird sensation came over me and he thrusted a couple more times inside of me.

I moaned loudly and clutched his back. I had not known sex between a woman and man could feel like this.

About the Author

Brittani Williams was born and raised in Philadelphia, PA, where she currently resides. She began writing when a school assignment required her to write a short play. This assignment showed her how far her imagination could go.

The last two years have definitely been a blessing for Brittani with the release of Daddy's Little Girl and tons of great feedback from readers all over. She has had the opportunity to participate in two anthology projects Fantasy and Flexin' & Sexin' with some of the hottest authors in the game. With the release of Sugar Walls she will have four projects in circulation, all released in the same year.

Brittani graciously thanks Mark Anthony and the entire Q-Boro staff for giving her the opportunity to show the world what her family and friends have raved about since day one.

Brittani is the mother of a four-year-old and is currently hard at work on her third and fourth novels. Stay Tuned for Brittani in 2008!

Acknowledgments

Wow, book number two and I thank God for the opportunity. I dedicate everything that I do to my wonderful son Kristion and I hope you know that all of my hard work is for you. My mom and dad who have supported me tremendously throughout this process I love you both with all of my heart and I'm glad that you believe in me. Curt, thanks for promoting me and selling my books! I appreciate all of your support and I'm glad that I have you standing behind me. To my cousin Peaches who I love dearly, thanks for all of the encouragement and your phone calls to say I love you. To all of my other family members I love you all and thanks for the support.

To Jennifer B, thanks for posting my postcards on your runs, it is your promotion that helps me sell books and I definitely appreciate that. I love you.

To my Pink Lace ENT girls, Jennifer, Nikki & Bebe, thanks for being such good friends and taking on a business venture with me. Though I know things were rough, I appreciate you all standing behind me.

To my special friend Buck Wild, thanks for all of the support and encouragement and thanks for believing in me when I didn't believe in myself. I will always love you for that if nothing else.

To Angie, thanks for promoting me all around the hospital, I feel so blessed to have someone like you around. To all of my other friends Ebey, Big Lil, Mike, Pat S, Ambi, April, Ang, Christina, Andre, and anyone that I have forgotten. I love you all.

To all of the people that have helped me promote either my book or my promotion company, Meastr'o ENT, Steve & Darrell, It is what it is ENT, Familia Facez, Flyata Designs and Rell 1800, thanks for all of your help. It is greatly appreciated.

To all of my co-workers, thanks so much for standing behind me and pushing me to keep going. I hope you all are proud of me.

Mark Anthony, I'm so glad that you gave me the chance to shine. You believed in my project and even when I doubted it, you didn't. I couldn't ask for a better boss and I appreciate everything that you've done for me. We're going to kill 'em this time!

Nakea Murray, thanks for all of the help and the knowledge that you have given me. When I needed someone to talk to you've always been there for me and I'm glad to have you in my life as a friend as well as professionally. I don't think that I've realized my full potential but I'm glad that you've always believed in me.

K. Elliot, thanks for my spot in *Fantasy* and **Azarel** thanks for my spot in *Flexin and Sexin*. You both have given me more chances to shine. I now have 4 projects in rotation at the same time, in one year! Thanks a bunch.

Anna J, girl I'm glad that you're always there to tell my crazy stories to and be a great friend when I need one.

K'wan, my homie, I've learned a lot from you and trust me, I've retained it all. You are the bomb and I hope to reach your level one day.

Erick S. Gray, you have been an inspiration and I thank you for being so humble. **Miasha,** you have always been so sweet and I'm so happy for you and all of you're accomplishments girl keep up the good work. To all of the other authors that I've come in contact with Daaimah S. Poole, Dejon, Andrea Blackstone, Zane, Allison Hobbs, Nicolette, Danette Majette, Donna Hill, Mika Miller, Hickson, Treasure E. Blue, and Latrese Carter, you all are an inspiration to me.

Karim Muhammed, you are the best photographer in the world. Thanks for taking such wonderful pictures of me.

To the **As the Page Turns Book Club** members, thanks for being so honest and supporting me with my book. I'm so glad that I decided to join such an exciting group. To all of the other book clubs out there, I believe I speak for all authors when I say we appreciate the support.

All of my readers, I am going to keep them coming so look out for me in 2008. I'm working on something big. To everyone that has stopped by www.brittani-williams.com and www.mypace.com/msbgw all of your comments keep me going. I promise that I won't disappoint you.

To all those that I didn't name, again charge it to my mind and not my heart. To those that believe in me and even those that don't I'm going to prove my point one way or another. It is definitely my time to shine!

Brittani

NOW AVAILABLE FROM

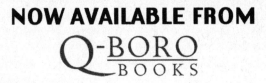

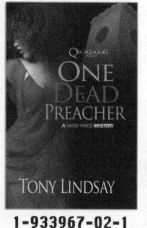

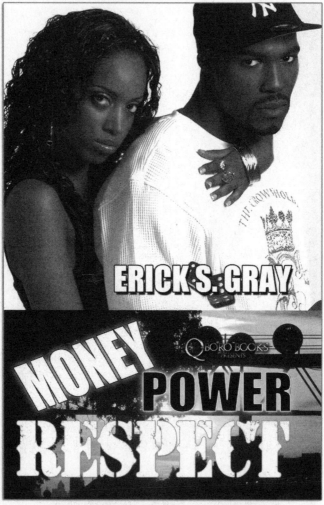